RAVE REVIEWS FOR
THE DEATH ARTIST AND
DENNIS ETCHISON!

"Exquisitely well written and stunningly original, these stories serve as fine examples of the ever-evolving literature of horror."

—*Publishers Weekly* (starred review)

"Etchison is one hell of a fiction writer."

—Stephen King

"This is an author who ranks among the finest short story writers of our day. *The Death Artist* is one of the best collections of this or any year."

—*Horror Online*

"Dennis Etchison is absolutely one of horror's most exciting, most radical and innovative talents."

—Peter Straub

"Etchison is one of the most accomplished practitioners of modern horror. And you don't have to worry about reading this book in the dark hours to ensure the right atmosphere; *The Death Artist* will get you anytime, anywhere."

—*Prism*

"No one can beat Etchison at generating an atmosphere of dread from the smallest, most seemingly inconsequential details. I don't often call a book essential; this one is."

—Fiona Webster, *Horror Garage*

MORE PRAISE FOR DENNIS ETCHISON!

Other *Leisure* books by
Dennis Etchison:
THE MUSEUM OF HORRORS

DENNIS ETCHISON

THE DEATH ARTIST

LEISURE BOOKS   NEW YORK CITY

A LEISURE BOOK®

February 2002

Published by

Dorchester Publishing Co., Inc.
276 Fifth Avenue
New York, NY 10001

ISBN 0-8439-4967-8

The name "Leisure Books" and the stylized "L" with design are trademarks of Dorchester Publishing Co., Inc.

Printed in the United States of America.

Visit us on the web at www.dorchesterpub.com.

To Theodore Sturgeon

TABLE OF CONTENTS

THE DEATH ARTIST

You have seen him but you did not recognize him. When he passed you on the street you would not look his way. He stood with you in the line and took a seat as the lights went down but when you heard his footsteps later, going home, you told yourself he was not there. He is the one who sent the letter, the one on the telephone who never speaks, the one who waits behind the door. He stops for every accident and never turns away from the chalk marks and the blood, for there is a lifemap in each dying and if he does not see it all his portraits will not be true. He wants to pass it on, the laughter and the cry in the night, so much the same at the end. It is not a hobby or a diversion. It is a method and an esthetic and a religion. He does not seek to convert you. He only wants you to know. He thinks you are ready. He is an artist and his subject is the high and the low rather than what lies between. You do not have to find him. He has already found you.

The Dog Park

Madding heard the dogs before he saw them.

They were snarling at each other through the hurricane fence, gums wet and incisors bared, as if about to snap the chain links that held them apart. A barrel-chested boxer reared and slobbered, driving a much smaller Australian kelpie away from the outside of the gate. Spittle flew and the links vibrated and rang.

A few seconds later their owners came running, barking commands and waving leashes like whips.

"Easy, boy," Madding said, reaching one hand out to the seat next to him. Then he remembered that he no longer had a dog of his own. There was nothing to worry about.

Dennis Etchison

He set the brake, rolled the window up all the way, locked the car and walked across the lot to the park.

The boxer was far down the slope by now, pulled along by a man in a flowered shirt and pleated trousers. The Australian sheepdog still trembled by the fence. Its owner, a young woman, jerked a choke chain.

"Greta, sit!"

As Madding neared the gate, the dog growled and tried to stand.

She yanked the chain harder and slapped its hindquarters back into position.

"Hello, Greta," said Madding, lifting the steel latch. He smiled at the young woman. "You've got a brave little dog there."

"I don't know why she's acting this way," she said, embarrassed.

"Is this her first time?"

"Pardon?"

"At the Dog Park."

"Yes . . ."

"It takes some getting used to," he told her. "All the freedom. They're not sure how to behave."

"Did you have the same trouble?"

"Of course." He savored the memory, and at the same time wanted to put it out of his mind. "Everybody does. It's normal."

"I named her after Garbo—you know, the ac-

16

tress? I don't think she likes crowds." She looked around. "Where's your dog?"

"Down there, I hope." Madding opened the gate and let himself in, then held it wide for her.

She was squinting at him. "Excuse me," she said, "but you work at Tri-Mark, don't you?"

Madding shook his head. "I'm afraid not."

The kelpie dragged her down the slope with such force that she had to dig her feet into the grass to stop. The boxer was nowhere in sight.

"Greta, heel!"

"You can let her go," Madding said as he came down behind her. "The leash law is only till three o'clock."

"What time is it now?"

He checked his watch. "Almost five."

She bent over and unfastened the leash from the ring on the dog's collar. She was wearing white cotton shorts and a plain, loose-fitting top.

"Did I meet you in Joel Silver's office?" she said.

"I don't think so." He smiled again. "Well, you and Greta have fun."

He wandered off, tilting his face back and breathing deeply. The air was moving, scrubbed clean by the trees, rustling the shiny leaves as it circulated above the city, exchanging pollutants for fresh oxygen. It was easier to be on his own, but without a dog to pick the direction he was at loose ends. He felt the loss tugging at him like a cord that had not yet been broken.

The park was only a couple of acres, nestled between the high, winding turns of a mountain road on one side and a densely overgrown canyon on the other. This was the only park where dogs were allowed to run free, at least during certain hours, and in a few short months it had become an unofficial meeting place for people in the entertainment industry. Where once pitches had been delivered in detox clinics and the gourmet aisles of Westside supermarkets, now ambitious hustlers frequented the Dog Park to sharpen their networking skills. Here starlets connected with recently divorced producers, agents jockeyed for favor with young executives on the come, and actors and screenwriters exchanged tips about veterinarians, casting calls and pilots set to go to series in the fall. All it took was a dog, begged, borrowed or stolen, and the kind of desperate gregariousness that causes one to press business cards into the hands of absolute strangers.

He saw dozens of dogs, expensive breeds mingling shamelessly with common mutts, a microcosm of democracy at work. An English setter sniffed an unshorn French poodle, then gave up and joined the pack gathered around a honey-colored cocker spaniel. A pair of black Great Dane puppies tumbled over each other golliwog-style, coming to rest at the feet of a tall, humorless German shepherd. An Afghan chased a Russian wolfhound. And there were the masters, posed against tree trunks, lounging at picnic tables, nervously cleaning up after their pets with long-handled scoopers while they waited to see who would enter the park next.

Madding played a game, trying to match up the animals with their owners. A man with a crewcut tossed a Frisbee, banking it against the setting sun like a translucent UFO before a bull terrier snatched it out of the air. Two fluffed Pekingese waddled across the path in front of Madding, trailing colorful leashes; when they neared the gorge at the edge of the park he started after them reflexively, then stopped as a short, piercing sound turned them and brought them back this way. A bodybuilder in a formfitting T-shirt glowered nearby, a silver whistle showing under his trimmed moustache.

Ahead, a Labrador, a chow and a schnauzer had a silkie cornered by a trash bin. Three people seated on a wooden bench glanced up, laughed, and returned to the curled script they were reading. Madding could not see the title, only that the cover was a bilious yellow-green.

"I know," said the young woman, drawing even with him, as her dog dashed off in an ever-widening circle. "It was at New Line. That was you, wasn't it?"

"I've never been to New Line," said Madding.

"Are you sure? The office on Robertson?"

"I'm sure."

"Oh." She was embarrassed once again, and tried to cover it with a self-conscious cheerfulness, the mark of a private person forced into playing the extrovert in order to survive. "You're not an actor, then?"

"Only a writer," said Madding.

She brightened. "I knew it!"

"Isn't everyone in this town?" he said. "The butcher, the baker, the kid who parks your car. . . . My drycleaner says he's writing a script for Tim Burton."

"Really?" she said, quite seriously. "I'm writing a spec script."

Oh no, he thought. He wanted to sink down into the grass and disappear among the ants and beetles, but the ground was damp from the sprinklers and her dog was circling, hemming him in.

"Sorry," he said.

"That's okay. I have a real job, too. I'm on staff at Fox Network."

"What show?" he asked, to be polite.

"*C.H.U.M.P.* The first episode is on next week. They've already ordered nine more, in case *Don't Worry, Be Happy* gets canceled."

"I've heard of it," he said.

"Have you? What have you heard?"

He racked his brain. "It's a cop series, right?"

"Canine-Human Unit, Metropolitan Police. You know, dogs that ride around in police cars, and the men and women they sacrifice themselves for? It has a lot of human interest, like *L.A. Law*, only it's told through the dogs' eyes."

"Look Who's Barking," he said.

"Sort of." She tilted her head to one side and thought for a moment. "I'm sorry," she said. "That was a joke, wasn't it?"

"Sort of."

"I get it." She went on. "But what I really want to write is Movies-of-the-Week. My agent says she'll put my script on Paul Nagle's desk, as soon as I have a first draft."

"What's it about?"

"It's called *A Little-Known Side of Elvis*. That's the working title. My agent says anything about Elvis will sell."

"Which side of Elvis is this one?"

"Well, for example, did you know about his relationships with dogs? Most people don't. *Hound Dog* wasn't just a song."

Her kelpie began to bark. A man with inflatable tennis shoes and a baseball cap worn backwards approached them, a clipboard in his hand.

Dennis Etchison

"Hi!" he said, all teeth. "Would you take a minute to sign our petition?"

"No problem," said the young woman. "What's it for?"

"They're trying to close the park to outsiders, except on weekends."

She took his ballpoint pen and balanced the clipboard on her tanned forearm. "How come?"

"It's the residents. They say we take up too many parking spaces on Mulholland. They want to keep the canyon for themselves."

"Well," she said, "they better watch out, or we might just start leaving our dogs here. Then they'll multiply and take over!"

She grinned, her capped front teeth shining in the sunlight like two chips of paint from a pearly-white Lexus.

"What residents?" asked Madding.

"The homeowners," said the man in the baseball cap, hooking a thumb over his shoulder.

Madding's eyes followed a line to the cliffs overlooking the park, where the cantilevered back-ends of several designer houses hung suspended above the gorge. The undersides of the decks, weathered and faded, were almost camouflaged by the weeds and chaparral.

"How about you?" The man took back the clipboard and held it out to Madding. "We need all the help we can get."

"I'm not a registered voter," said Madding.

"You're not?"

"I don't live here," he said. "I mean, I did, but I don't now. Not anymore."

"Are *you* registered?" the man asked her.

"Yes."

"In the business?"

"I work at Fox," she said.

"Oh, yeah? How's the new regime? I hear Lili put all the old-timers out to pasture."

"Not the studio," she said. "The network."

"Really? Do you know Kathryn Baker, by any chance?"

"I've seen her parking space. Why?"

"I used to be her dentist." The man took out his wallet. "Here, let me give you my card."

"That's all right," she said. "I already have someone."

"Well, hold onto it anyway. You never know. Do you have a card?"

She reached into a Velcro pouch at her waist and handed him a card with a quill pen embossed on one corner.

The man read it. " '*C.H. U.M.P.*'—that's great! Do you have a dental adviser yet?"

"I don't think so."

"Could you find out?"

"I suppose."

He turned to Madding. "Are you an actor?"

"Writer. But not the kind you mean."

The man was puzzled. The young woman

looked at him blankly. Madding felt the need to explain himself.

"I had a novel published, and somebody bought an option. I moved down here to write the screenplay."

"Title?" said the man.

"You've probably never heard of it," said Madding. "It was called *And Soon the Night*."

"That's it!" she said. "I just finished reading it—I saw your picture on the back of the book!" She furrowed her brow, a slight dimple appearing on the perfectly smooth skin between her eyes, as she struggled to remember. "Don't tell me. Your name is . . ."

"David Madding," he said, holding out his hand.

"Hi!" she said. "I'm Stacey Chernak."

"Hi, yourself."

"Do you have a card?" the man said to him.

"I'm all out," said Madding. It wasn't exactly a lie. He had never bothered to have any printed.

"What's the start date?"

"There isn't one," said Madding. "They didn't renew the option."

"I see," said the man in the baseball cap, losing interest.

A daisy chain of small dogs ran by, a miniature collie chasing a longhaired dachshund chasing a shivering Chihuahua. The collie blurred as it went past, its long coat streaking like a flame.

"Well, I gotta get some more signatures before dark. Don't forget to call me," the man said to her. "I can advise on orthodontics, accident reconstruction, anything they want."

"How about animal dentistry?" she said.

"Hey, why not?"

"I'll give them your name."

"Great," he said to her. "Thanks!"

"Do you think that's his collie?" she said when he had gone.

Madding considered. "More likely the Irish setter."

They saw the man lean down to hook his fingers under the collar of a golden retriever. From the back, his baseball cap revealed the emblem of the New York Yankees. Not from around here, Madding thought. But then, who is?

"Close," she said, and laughed.

The man led his dog past a dirt mound, where there was a drinking fountain and a spigot that ran water into a trough for the animals.

"Water," she said. "That's a good idea. Greta!"

The kelpie came bounding over, eager to escape the attentions of a randy pit bull. They led her to the mound. As Greta drank, Madding read the sign over the spigot:

CAUTION
WATCH OUT FOR MOUNTAIN LIONS

"What do you think that means?" she said. "It isn't true, is it?"

Madding felt a tightness in his chest. "It could be. This is still wild country."

"Greta, stay with me . . ."

"Don't worry. They only come out at night, probably."

"Where's your dog?" she said.

"I wish I knew."

She tilted her head, uncertain whether or not he was making another joke.

"He ran away," Madding told her.

"When?"

"Last month. I used to bring him here all the time. One day he didn't come when I called. It got dark, and they closed the park, but he never came back."

"Oh, I'm so sorry!"

"Yeah, me too."

"What was his name?"

"He didn't have one. I couldn't make up my mind, and then it was too late."

They walked on between the trees. She kept a close eye on Greta. Somewhere music was playing. The honey-colored cocker spaniel led the German shepherd, the Irish setter and a dalmation to a redwood table. There the cocker's owner, a woman with brassy hair and a sagging green halter, poured white wine into plastic cups for several men.

"I didn't know," said Stacey.

"I missed him at first, but now I figure he's better off. Someplace where he can run free, all the time."

"I'm sorry about your dog," she said. "That's so sad. But what I meant was, I didn't know you were famous."

It was hard to believe that she knew the book. The odds against it were staggering, particularly considering the paltry royalties. He decided not to ask what she thought of it. That would be pressing his luck.

"Who's famous? I sold a novel. Big deal."

"Well, at least you're a *real* writer. I envy you."

"Why?"

"You have it made."

Sure I do, thought Madding. One decent review in the *Village Voice Literary Supplement*, and some reader at a production company makes an inquiry, and the next thing I know my agent makes a deal with all the money in the world at the top of a ladder. Only the ladder doesn't go far enough. And now I'm back to square one, the option money used up, with a screenplay written on spec that's not worth what it cost me to Xerox it, and I'm six months behind on the next novel. But I've got it made. Just ask the IRS.

The music grew louder as they walked. It seemed to be coming from somewhere overhead. Madding gazed up into the trees, where the late-afternoon rays sparkled through the leaves, gold coins edged in blackness. He thought he heard voices, too, and the clink of glasses. Was there a party? The entire expanse of the park was visible from here, but he could see no evidence of a large group anywhere. The sounds were diffused and unlocalized, as if played back through widely spaced, out-of-phase speakers.

"Where do you live?" she asked.

"What?"

"You said you don't live here anymore."

"In Calistoga."

"Where's that?"

"Up north."

"Oh."

He began to relax. He was glad to be finished with this town.

"I closed out my lease today," he told her. "Everything's packed. As soon as I hit the road, I'm out of here."

"Why did you come back to the park?"

A good question, he thought. He hadn't planned to stop by. It was a last-minute impulse.

"I'm not sure," he said. No, that wasn't true. He might as well admit it. "It sounds crazy, but I guess I wanted to look for my dog. I thought

I'd give it one more chance. It doesn't feel right, leaving him."

"Do you think he's still here?"

He felt a tingling in the pit of his stomach. It was not a good feeling. I shouldn't have come, he thought. Then I wouldn't have had to face it. It's dangerous here, too dangerous for there to be much hope.

"At least I'll know," he said.

He heard a sudden intake of breath and turned to her. There were tears in her eyes, as clear as diamonds.

"It's like the end of your book," she said. "When the little girl is alone, and doesn't know what's going to happen next . . ."

My God, he thought, she did read it. He felt flattered, but kept his ego in check. She's not so tough. She has a heart, after all, under the bravado. That's worth something—it's worth a lot. I hope she makes it, the Elvis script, whatever she really wants. She deserves it.

She composed herself and looked around, blinking. "What *is* that?"

"What's what?"

"Don't you hear it?" She raised her chin and moved her head from side to side, eyes closed.

She meant the music, the glasses, the sound of the party that wasn't there.

"I don't know."

Now there was the scraping of steel somewhere behind them, like a rough blade drawn through metal. He stopped and turned around quickly.

A couple of hundred yards away, at the top of the slope, a man in a uniform opened the gate to the park. Beyond the fence, a second man climbed out of an idling car with a red, white and blue shield on the door. He had a heavy chain in one hand.

"Come on," said Madding. "It's time to go."

"It can't be."

"The security guards are here. They close the park at six."

"Already?"

Madding was surprised, too. He wondered how long they had been walking. He saw the man with the crewcut searching for his Frisbee in the grass, the bull terrier at his side. The group on the bench and the woman in the halter were collecting their things. The bodybuilder marched his two ribboned Pekingese to the slope. The Beverly Hills dentist whistled and stood waiting for his dog to come to him. Madding snapped to, as if waking up. It really was time.

The sun had dropped behind the hills and the grass under his feet was darkening. The car in the parking lot above continued to idle; the rumbling of the engine reverberated in the natural bowl of the park, as though close enough to bulldoze them out of the way. He heard a rhythm in the throbbing, and realized that it was music, after all.

They had wandered close to the edge, where the park ended and the gorge began. Over the gorge, the deck of one of the cantilevered houses beat like a drum.

"Where's Greta?" she said.

He saw the stark expression, the tendons outlined through the smooth skin of her throat.

"Here, girl! Over here . . . !"

She called out, expecting to see her dog. Then she clapped her hands together. The sound bounced back like the echo of a gunshot from the depths of the canyon. The dog did not come.

In the parking lot, the second security guard let a Doberman out of the car. It was a sleek, black streak next to him as he carried the heavy chain to his partner, who was waiting for the park to empty before padlocking the gate.

Madding took her arm. Her skin was covered with gooseflesh. She drew away.

"I can't go," she said. "I have to find Greta."

He scanned the grassy slopes with her, avoiding the gorge until there was nowhere left to look. It was blacker than he remembered. Misshapen bushes and stunted shrubs filled the canyon below, extending all the way down to the formal boundaries of the city. He remembered standing here only a few weeks ago, in

31

exactly the same position. He had told himself then that his dog could not have gone over the edge, but now he saw that there was nowhere else to go.

The breeze became a wind in the canyon and the black liquid eye of a swimming pool winked at him from far down the hillside. Above, the sound of the music stopped abruptly.

"You don't think she went down there, do you?" said Stacey. There was a catch in her voice. "The mountain lions . . ."

"They only come out at night."

"But it *is* night!"

They heard a high, broken keening.

"Listen!" she said. "That's Greta!"

"No, it's not. Dogs don't make that sound. It's—" He stopped himself.

"*What?*"

"Coyotes."

He regretted saying it.

Now, without the music, the shuffling of footsteps on the boards was clear and unmistakable. He glanced up. Shadows appeared over the edge of the deck as a line of heads gathered to look down. Ice cubes rattled and someone laughed. Then someone else made a shushing sound and the silhouetted heads bobbed silently, listening and watching.

Can they see us? he wondered.

Madding felt the presence of the Doberman

behind him, at the top of the slope. How long would it take to close the distance, once the guards set it loose to clear the park? Surely they would call out a warning first. He waited for the voice, as the seconds ticked by on his watch.

"I have to go get her," she said, starting for the gorge.

"No . . ."

"I can't just leave her."

"It's not safe," he said.

"But she's down there, I know it! Greta!"

There was a giggling from the deck.

They can hear us, too, he thought. Every sound, every word magnified, like a Greek amphitheater. Or a Roman one.

Rover, Spot, Towser? No, Cubby. That's what I was going to call you, if there had been time. I always liked the name. *Cubby*.

He made a decision.

"Stay here," he said, pushing her aside.

"Where are you going?"

"I'm going over."

"You don't have to. It's my dog . . ."

"Mine, too."

Maybe they're both down there, he thought.

"I'll go with you," she said.

"No."

He stood there, thinking, It all comes down to this. There's no way to avoid it. There never was.

Dennis Etchison

"But you don't know what's there . . . !"

"Go," he said to her, without turning around. "Get out of here while you can. There's still time."

Go home, he thought, wherever that is. You have a life ahead of you. It's not too late, if you go right now, without looking back.

"Wait . . . !"

He disappeared over the edge.

A moment later there was a new sound, something more than the breaking of branches and the thrashing. It was powerful and deep, followed immediately by a high, mournful yipping. Then there was only silence, and the night.

From above the gorge, a series of quick, hard claps fell like rain.

It was the people on the deck.

They were applauding.

The Last Reel

As soon as I saw her face, I knew where I was.

I'd been lost in the canyons, looking for a sign, and after a while all I wanted was out. I couldn't even read the map book. The dome light flickered like a firefly in a jar and the street-lamps were hidden behind a scrim of leaves and branches. If there really was a street called Rose Petal Lane I couldn't find it.

Then I made the turn onto Sierra Vista and there she was, bigger than life.

It was hard to judge distances but she must have been about a half-mile away, floating through the darkness over the trees that pointed toward the old reservoir at the top. From here I figured her face was at least ten feet tall, which made her mouth roughly the size of an open manhole. I didn't want to think about the rest of her. But I had come this far—what was the point in turning back now?

I downshifted, grinding the gears, and kept moving.

The sky grew bright with the glow of her skin and the waterfall of blond hair around her face. Her head bobbed up and down like a flesh-colored zeppelin looking for a place to land. As I got closer there were other colors, too, drifting in and out of a long beam of light trained on the reservoir wall. The numbers were worn off the curb but I knew I had found Donn Hedgeman's house. Who else would use the side of the Stone River Dam for a movie screen? I'd heard that his parties were legendary. The man had outdone himself this time.

I had to park halfway back down the canyon. Porsches and Jags and Mercedes-Benzes were wedged halfway across every driveway between here and Sunset. Walking up, I saw two college boys in red vests on one of the sidestreets, waving flashlights like ushers at a movie premiere. Somehow I had missed the valet parking. It was just as well. My Toyota hadn't been washed in months.

On foot, I could have found Donn's house with my eyes closed. It was only eight o'clock but already the voices were so loud they might have been screaming, trapped in the canyon and magnified by the concrete dam at the end. Over the top of a redwood fence I noticed a sea of blond coifs, all the same color as the one in the sky. I opened the gate and let myself into the backyard, looking around for Donn.

"Skippy!"

I ignored the voice and kept walking as if I knew where I was going. There was a kidney-shaped swimming pool lit by underwater floodlights, and a pink shape wavered near the bottom, distorted by the ripples. A group of men gathered around the edge, some in jackets and ties, others in T-shirts and jeans. They cheered as the swimmer surfaced, borne up by an inflated life jacket. Then I realized there was no life jacket. It was her breasts that were inflated. She arched her body, as if hoping to thrust her nipples high enough to catch the beam of the projector, then threw her head back and dove again, the polished lips of her vagina cleaving the water. The men hooted and applauded. I worked my way around the pool, heading across the patio.

"Skippy?"

There was a burst of flashguns inside the house, turning the glass walls of the rec room blue-white. I spotted a man with huge, frizzy hair next to a billiard table, surrounded by photographers. It had to be Donn.

Dennis Etchison

Now someone grabbed my arm. I felt my elbow caught between two balloons, as if held there by static electricity. I tried to shake them off and glanced over my shoulder.

A stunningly beautiful young woman clutched my arm to her bosom. Her vinyl dress was cut so low it looked like two bald men were trying to fight their way out the front.

"You *are!*" She got a look at my face and dug her long black fingernails into my sweater. "I knew it . . . !"

"Hi."

"I had the biggest crush on you!" She did not want to let go of my arm. "You were a *lot* cuter than that other dude, the one who played your brother . . ."

"Tony."

I could have told her all about Tony Sargent. How he ended up with a habit so big he couldn't get a job pushing a broom at the studio, how he started knocking off liquor stores with his old lady's pantyhose pulled over his head, and how he blew his brains out the night she o.d.'d on the last of his smack. I didn't want to burst her bubble. The show had been out of production since the late seventies but the reruns wouldn't quit. As far as she was concerned I was still Skippy Boomer. She was not alone. At least she hadn't asked for my autograph. Not yet.

"Was that his name?"

"Good old Tony," I said. "A great guy." I nodded at the rec room, the way I learned to do it in acting class: the gesture first, then the line. "Is that Donn?"

"Which one was he?"

"The Hedge Man," I said. "This is his party, isn't it?"

"Oh yeah." Her face fell and I thought I caught a glimpse of something fading out behind the layers of makeup, something almost sad. Then she blinked at me, fluttering her false eyelashes. *"You* know *Donn?"*

"Who doesn't?"

"He's such a trip! I'd work for him anytime . . ."

"Excuse me," I told her, retrieving my arm. "I have to say hello."

I made my way across the patio. The actress in the sky was emoting with mounting fervor, closing her shiny eyelids and tossing her head from side to side as if lost in an opium dream, but no one seemed to be watching. I saw an old theater projector set up on the buffet table, with several film cans stacked next to it. The reel that was on now appeared to be near its end. I opened the sliding glass door and slipped inside, as the tail of the film clattered onto the takeup spool and the beam of light went white.

Donn was in the middle of an interview. A man with tattooed arms and a baseball cap squinted into a Hi-8 videocam and stammered through a list of prepared questions, while three ridiculously gorgeous women stood on the sidelines and laughed at each of Donn's jokes. He was the center of attention, as always.

"What's your next project?" I heard the young man ask.

"*Magic Fingers Motel*, for Vulcano Video."

The women whooped and clapped their hands.

"Starring?"

"Lo Ryder," said Donn without missing a beat, "Charmin, Kerry O'Quim . . . How's *that* for a cast? Did I leave anyone out?"

"Rosie Gates!" shouted a beauty in leather hotpants.

Donn snapped his fingers and nodded, rolling his eyes.

"Yeah, Rosie! Wait'll you see the tush on that girl! I met her at the F.O.X.E. Awards. Says d.p.'s not enough—she wants to do *triple* penetration! Maybe I'll let Rocco break her in!"

The gorgeous women cracked up.

"Anything else?"

"Lemme see. *The Ram Doubler, Seven Come Eleven, Close Shavers Part Two*, another *Bun Boy's Big Adventure* . . . and of course *WetWork*, starring the fabulous Celestine Prophet!"

Donn shot a glance outside. Now only an empty square of light showed in the sky.

"What the *fuck?*" He put his hand up, blocking the lens of the camera. "That's a wrap."

He brushed past me on his way out to the patio.

"Hey, Skipper," he said under his breath. "Stay right where you are. We got business to talk about . . ."

The gorgeous women started out after him. A fourth, who couldn't have been more than eighteen, had been lingering in the background, watching from the hallway. Now she stepped out of the shadows and followed tentatively, as though afraid to be seen. She hesitated by the door.

"Excuse me," she said shyly, "but can I ask you something?"

"Sure," I said.

"Are . . . are you an actor?"

Busted again. "I used to be."

"I thought so." She kept her head down, too nervous to meet my eyes. "*The Boomer Family* was my favorite, when I was little."

"Thanks," I said, and almost meant it.

She didn't look like she belonged at the party. She had on a simple summer dress with a high neckline and low-heeled pumps, no jewelry except for a small gold heart on a chain around her neck and hardly any makeup. She didn't need it. She stood next to me and watched the commotion outside.

Donn was flapping his arms and chewing out a guy in ragged cutoffs who was supposed to be running the projector. For a moment I thought he was going to slap the kid across the face, in front of everyone.

"What's your name?" I said.

"Charlene."

"Hi, Charlene. I'm Rob." I held out my hand and finally had to touch her wrist before she would look at me.

"I know. Rob Miller."

That was a surprise. Most people think my name's Skippy, even though that was only the character I played.

She grinned as she took her hand away from mine, embarrassed. Behind her, on the patio, women with matching turned-up noses and collagen lips leaned over the projector, allowing Donn to audition their perfect breasts while they helped him load the next reel.

"What are you doing here?" I asked.

"What?"

"I mean, where are you from?"

"Jonesville," she said. "That's in Iowa."

"Did you come out here to go to school?"

"Not really. I want to be an actor."

She sounded like she meant it. "That's a tough gig," I told her. "Are you taking classes?"

"I was, back home."

"Do you have an agent yet?"

"I just got one."

"Good," I said. "What's his name?"

"Jim Western."

That sounded familiar but I couldn't place it. "Who's he with?"

"Global Modeling," she said, "on La Cienega. Have you heard of them?"

I had. They represented most of the nude models and dancers in town, and provided the talent for Vulcano, Silver Nitro and VibroFlix, the largest producers of triple-X films and videos in the San Fernando Valley. I didn't know what to say.

"That's how I met Donn," she explained.

I nodded as if I understood.

"Why don't you try Dimension Films, over at Miramax? They might have something for you." I racked my brain to remember who else was making lowbudget features at the moment, hoping to come up with a legitimate alternative. "Or TriMark. Or Full Moon. You'll probably have to do horror movies at first, but at least it's a start."

"I already have one lined up," she said, without a trace of pretension. "It might be a series, if it's successful. They're writing the script right now. It's called *The Last Whorehouse on the Left*."

At that moment the white light outside darkened and the enormous face of Donn's newest contract player, Celestine Prophet, reappeared on the side of the dam above the treetops. Her mouth was open but it was not empty. A hoot went up from the crowd. Two starlets with impossible figures stepped out of their skintight dresses, dove into the deep end and began rolling through the water like dolphins locked in a slippery embrace, as the man with the video camera hurried out to record the action.

"I don't know if I can do it," Charlene said softly.

"Maybe you shouldn't," I said.

"Not the way they do." She meant the starlets outside, those in the pool and the others with their synthetic bodies and sparkling clothes and desperate recklessness. "Should I change my name, do you think?"

"Why? I like Charlene."

"Oh, that's not my real name . . ."

Donn was on his way back in. As I moved aside, she took my hand and clasped it tightly to her side. I felt the youthful firmness of her body moving beneath the thin cotton and realized that she was trembling. She leaned close and whispered in my ear.

"*Help me.*"

"How?" I said, without moving my lips, as Donn approached the glass doors.

"Not here."

Donn hadn't met my eyes yet. He was squeezing the buttocks of the one in the hotpants. He twitched his fuzzy moustache, made an O with his mouth and sucked air, moaning in ecstasy.

"Where?" I said.

"Later. I'll find you . . ."

She separated from me and disappeared into the hall.

Donn entertained the troops in the rec room. I stood by while he told a story about a guy who became famous for having his penis cut off twice. I'd heard it before, the day I met him in the lobby of the SAG building, where he held forth with a slightly different version of the same routine. He had recognized me and later, over a drink, offered me a chance to direct. I didn't know who he was then but I found out. I came to his party because he claimed that plenty of regular industry people moonlight in the adult biz under other names, and he threw around numbers that added up to more money than I had made from a whole season on CBS when I was a kid. That was all gone now, of course; there weren't any decent residual clauses back then. I hadn't had many acting jobs since puberty, except for some sci-fi motocycle flicks and voiceovers on Saturday morning TV. *The Boomer Family* was a curse. My ex had thought she was marrying into show business but what she got was a part-time real estate agent. I couldn't hack it anymore, not after the divorce. Maybe Tony had seen the handwriting on the wall, after all.

Donn finished his story in the rec room and introduced the girls to the reporters from *Hustler's Erotic Video Guide* and *Adult Video News*. Then he caught my eye and nodded toward the hall that led to the rest of the house. As we got to the end of the hall I saw an open door and a bright bedroom, where at least two very naked young women were engaged in an act involving a dildo of life-threatening proportions. A videographer with a handheld BetaCam circled around them, offering unnecessary advice as to positions and techniques. Donn led me to the den.

"Strap this on for size," he said when he closed the door. " 'Geoffrey Nightshade.' "

"Who?"

"Your *non de plume*."

He took a swig from a Heineken's and smacked his lips, then set the bottle down and leaned back in the leather chair, eyelids at half-mast.

"We send out press releases, hinting that you're a famous European director. They'll beat their meat tryin' to nail you. Is it Karel Reisz? Dario Argento? Michaelangelo Fuckin' Antonioni?"

"Antonioni's in a wheelchair," I said. "He had a stroke."

"That's just it—we don't say! You're this artsy-fartsy schmuck who came here for some real action. You want to do NC-17 but the majors won't let you, blah blah blah. Maybe you're Brian Fuckin' DePalma, who the hell knows? Is it beautiful?"

"Except for one thing," I said. "Everybody knows what I look like."

"Don't be so conceited," he said.

That brought me up short. Right, I thought. But then I thought, He doesn't know what it's like. The red hair, the freckles . . . I couldn't even go to the 7-Eleven at two o'clock in the morning without hearing the name *Skippy!* behind my back. Once, in Vegas, the men's room attendant passed a piece of paper under the stall door and asked me to sign it.

"*You* recognized me," I said.

A faint smile curled his lips as he sat there watching me, his pupils black. What was he looking for? The weakness, I decided. The character flaw that he could exploit. It was what he used on the beauty pageant girls, the high school sweethearts he talked onto their backs in front of the camera, the way he turned their vanity against them until they ended up begging him for a chance to be a star. I wondered if it ever failed.

"Just kidding," he said. He winked, sat up and reached for a bowl of Doritos, stuffed his face reflexively and washed the chips down with the rest of the beer.

"So what would we do," I said, "shoot on a closed set?"

"There's ways. Secret locations, midnight to dawn . . ."

"What about the crew?"

"Wear a disguise. Pull a hat down over your eyes. Or a cape—that's it, like Dracula! He walks around with the collar up, nobody can see his face . . ."

He was indomitable. I had to admire the hustle. He was getting me to think about the possibilities. A few more minutes and I would be the one making the suggestions.

"Thanks, anyway," I told him. I started to get up. "But it just won't work."

"How does sixty thousand dollars sound?" he said calmly. "Plus a buck for every cassette sold."

"Don't jerk me around, Donn."

"I'm not! You don't know this business. Six thousand titles last year—a two-billion-dollar gross, just for the rentals! How many did the majors release? A hundred and ninety-seven. And two-thirds of those lost money. That's why Hollywood hates our ass."

"Sixty thousand," I said, letting it sink in. "For one video. Yeah, right."

He shook his head impatiently. "Not video—thirty-five millimeter. First class all the way. Say a series of three or four. We move twenty-five, thirty thousand copies each, list price, no sell-throughs. Plus a soft version for cable. You do the arithmetic."

I couldn't, but I knew it was enough to catch up on the alimony payments, settle with American Express and get the hell out of L.A.

"What kind of pictures are we talking about?" I said.

"Anything you want. *Anything*. I've got so many great ideas I don't have time to do 'em all."

He shrugged in the direction of a floor-to-ceiling bookcase filled with scripts. I made out some of the titles, written in marking pen on the edges: *Rumper Room, The Cunning Linguist, Ready Whipped, Gag Ball, Rocket to Uranus* . . .

I must have flinched as I read them, because he waved his hand dismissively.

"But what I really want to do is a crossover. Semi-legit. You can write it yourself. Whatever turns you on, as long as it's got the wood and the money shots."

"Like?"

"You name it. My cameraman worked with Orson Welles, my sound mixer's at Todd-AO, I got an editing bay at Foto-Kem . . . We're talking class, not some home movie with a mattress on the floor!"

He reached behind the chair and handed me several tapes as if dealing out a hand of cards.

"*Latex Dreams, The PsychoAnalist, Harry Butts in the Outback* . . . all directed by Peter Shooter." Donn looked at me expectantly.

I drew a blank on the name.

"You know who he really is, don't you? Drew Drake! The guy that does those perfume ads on TV? Lots of mood lighting, deep-focus—and the acting! Check out the stairway scene in *Gummy and Pokey*. Fay Way has six minutes of dialogue, no cuts, with Billy Backgate. Then they go right into a mish, a reverse cowgirl, around the world, and they finish with an inverted hole-in-one. Awesome!"

"Okay, okay . . ."

"And I can get you stars. How about Foxe Bleu? Or Oral Robert? Ever hear of Paul Riser? Take your pick—they *all* work for me. Not to mention Celestine Prophet! Now you know what *drop-dead gorgeous* means. You saw the movie, right?"

"Not yet. I just got here."

"Check it out. She's got a lot of potential. Vulcano wants her to beat the world gang-bang record, seven hundred guys in one day. Shit, she can do that, as long as they keep their fingers out of her—too many scratches. But I want her for something special first. Real class . . ."

"Why not get Drew Drake?"

"He's busy shooting that LaToya Jackson movie for Showtime. *Diana Ross Raw* or whever the hell it's called."

"Why me?"

"I'm a fan." He shrugged, as if stating the obvious. "So sue me."

"You don't even know if I can direct."

"You did three episodes of *Blossom*, two *Space Precincts* and one *Jaleel White Show*, before he flipped out."

He had done his homework.

"I was only first a.d. on those," I reminded him.

"But you know the drill. Three two-day shoots. Think you can handle a total of six fucking days?" He got up, went to his desk and opened a checkbook ledger. "I'll give you an advance. How much to seal the deal?"

"I don't know, Donn . . ."

"Say five large?" He scrawled his name on a check and tore it out of the book. "Think about it and call me. Just don't wait too long. I'm back in Australia next month for *Bun Boy Goes Down Under*."

In the hall ahead of me, a bimbo came out of the bathroom. She looked vaguely familiar. Her hair was teased and sprayed into a blond waterfall like the other girls. When she grabbed my hand I did a double-take.

"Charlene?" I said.

She wiped her nose with a tissue and pulled me into the bathroom. Her eyes were moist, as if she had been crying.

"Sorry," she said, closing and locking the door, "but I don't know who else to ask."

"That's all right. What—?"

"I've only been in the business for a month . . ."

She began to cry. First her wide, sky-blue eyes focused intently on my face, as if watching every shift in expression, every muscle tic, before deciding whether to go on. Apparently enough of what I was feeling showed, because she slumped against the door and lowered her face, wiping her nose again. When she raised her head the whites of her eyes were red and tears spilled out and ran down to her perfect nostrils and the cracked red skin there. She must have done a lot of crying lately. The tears dripped off the narrow point of her chin—too narrow, I noticed for the first time. She had already been to a plastic surgeon. Next would come the incisions under her small, flawless breasts, which might mean surgically repositioning the nipples, depending on the size of the implants.

"You can still get out," I said. "It's not too late."

"But I signed a contract."

"Contracts can be broken. I'll find you a lawyer . . ."

"You don't understand—I need the money. What am I going to do, go back to Jonesville and get a job at the phone company? Do you know what that pays? No way!"

She rubbed her nose, trying to compose herself.

"I really don't mind the work," she said. "I never had an orgasm before my first d.p., and I've done anal plenty of times, with my boyfriend. It's not so bad if you're lubed."

"How many pictures have you made?" I heard myself ask.

"Two, counting the one that isn't out yet."

"What's the name of the first one?"

"*WetWork*," she said. "Did you see it? Donn wants me to do a series next, if he can find the right actor-director."

"What do you mean?"

"A real actor, who can direct his own scenes . . ."

So that was what the sixty grand was for. He wanted to buy a face the public had seen before but never in porn. It was another stunt to generate publicity. I wondered how much Donn would offer George Clooney or Brad Pitt, if there was a chance he could get them.

"Excuse me."

She blocked my way, holding the doorknob behind her back.

"I don't mind the name, either. Celestine's pretty, don't you think? It's just that Donn won't let me use on the set, and I need something . . ."

"I have to go."

"Please?" She pressed against me and guided my hand up under her dress, so that I could feel the latex thong bikini she was already wearing, in preparation for her introduction to the press. "I can't make it straight. Do you have just a *little* coke? I'll be nice, you'll see . . ."

From the hall I heard Donn searching for his new starlet. I waited for him to pass, then lifted her off her feet. She was light as a plastic doll. I swung her around, set her down and opened the door.

As I ducked through the crowd in the rec room Donn was making excuses to buy a little more time. Then he went back into the hall. I heard him raise his voice and another voice sobbing. A minute later he returned and announced that Celestine Prophet was almost ready to make her entrance. Meanwhile, he reminded everybody, *WetWork* was running continuously outside. On the way down to the car I felt his check in my shirt pocket. It seemed to be pounding against my chest. I wondered whether he had made it out to Geoffrey Night-shade or Skippy Boomer. Either way I wouldn't be able to cash it, but I wasn't ready to look yet. In the sky a movie was ending or beginning, I couldn't tell which. I decided it didn't matter. The last reel would be just like the first.

When They Gave Us Memory

Halfway around the bay, before passing through the rock, he stopped and listened.

There was only the creaking of masts as sailboats listed back at the docks, straining their ropes and drubbing the pilings where they were moored. That and a distant hissing as water lapped the shore and deposited another layer of broken shells on the sand.

He saw the beach and the pier through the mist, the teenagers with zinc oxide on their noses, the white-legged tourists in walking shorts. No one else, except for the faded statue of an old-fashioned groom or footman in front of the carousel enclosure. The path along the jetty behind him was clear.

Even so, he could not shake the conviction that he was being followed.

He had sensed eyes on him in the restaurant, and the feeling grew when he went down to the pier. At every stand and gift shop he had paused, pretending interest in the souvenirs as he stole glances over his shoulder, but the boards remained empty. Pearly mobiles spinning in Mother Goose's Mall, cotton candy congealing against glass in the Taffy House, postcards curling outside the Fortune Hunter. Nothing else. He tried to let it go.

I should have called first, he thought.

He had hoped to surprise them in Captain Ahab's, their usual lunchtime spot, but the drive was longer than he remembered and he'd arrived late; by then strangers filled every table. Had his parents come early to avoid the noon rush and then gone for a walk? He couldn't imagine his dad sitting any longer than necessary. . . .

By now he had covered most of the waterfront, including the pier and the beach. All that was left was the jetty, a stone path that curved out over the bay in a half circle before returning to shore. In order to complete his search he would have to pass through the rock, an ancient landmark left untouched by the harbor's developers except for the installation of a railing where the foothold narrowed and became treacherous.

Now the natural arch loomed before him, dark and dripping with moisture.

He hesitated as a sudden wind moaned within the cavern.

Leaning on a coin-operated telescope, he caught his breath. Here the sea was calm, lapping gently at colonies of mollusks that clung to the slippery stones, at skittering crustaceans that sought purchase on the slick, eroded surfaces. Farther out, however, past the breakers, whitecaps were already forming where the currents merged in the gulf.

He watched one of the whitecaps detach from the tip of a wave, lift and begin to drift inland. Then another, another, flecks of spume breaking loose and taking flight.

They were coming this way.

When he saw that they were gulls, he waved. They swooped closer, poised just above the railing, their sleek wings fully extended.

Then they cawed, zeroing in on him.

He held out his arms to show that he had no food, no bread or leftover bait, but they dropped closer, feathers ruffling as they hovered in a holding pattern. The largest gull beat the air and cawed again. He noticed the sharp beak, the arrow tongue, the beady eyes focused on his empty fingers, and nervously stuffed his hands into his pockets.

The bird cocked its head, opened its beak wider, and shrieked.

What did it see?

He turned.

There was no one else on the jetty. A quarter mile away, the teenagers and tourists were still on the beach. The concession stands on the pier were boarded up now. It appeared that even the carousel was closed; the statue of the groom was no longer there.

When he turned back, the gulls were gone. He caught a last glimpse of their crescent wings pumping away on the horizon.

Ahead, a wave boomed in the cave.

The tide was rising. As plumes of spray settled over him he imagined the jetty awash, the rock path submerged, cutting off his return to land.

There was nothing left to do but go through before the waters rose any higher.

In the center of the arch a circle of diffused light shone through salt spray. The jetty beyond curved landward again so that there seemed to be nothing but endless sea on the other side. The walls of the cave swam with condensation, winking at him as though encrusted with tiny eyes.

He let go of the railing, hunched his shoulders, and walked forward.

Inside, the pounding of the surf was magnified until the pressure against his eardrums reached an all but unbearable level. He reconsidered, but there was no way around the rock. The jetty leading out from shore was less than a yard wide here, with only jagged boulders and the ocean beyond the railing. And the tide was swelling dangerously. Wasn't that a splash of white foam already bobbing above the path behind him?

Between the ebb and flow he heard water draining away, every drop resonating with the force of a pistol shot. He covered his ears but the throbbing was in the bones of his skull. He took his hands away, and almost lost his footing as a deep, bellowing roar sounded directly in front of him.

The cave wall shimmered and expanded, and something huge and formless spilled out over the rail into the circle of light, blocking his way.

A sea lion.

The massive creature reared its head, settled heavily on its haunches, and bellowed again.

He held the rail tightly and stood stock-still.

After a few seconds the animal twitched its glistening gray whiskers and waddled aside to allow passage. Another, smaller shape wriggled wetly in the shadows. It slapped its flippers and cried out hoarsely, as if welcoming him.

He took a breath, measuring his next step.

"Hi," said a voice.

He froze as something cold touched the middle of his back, then came to rest on his shoulder.

"I hope you don't mind," said the voice, barely audible above the pounding.

He spun around too fast. This time he lost his foothold and went sprawling.

A statue looked down at him. It was the groom from the pier. The cutaway jacket now hung in sodden folds. The figure extended a clammy, gloved hand and helped him to his feet.

"I hope you don't mind, but I recognized you right off."

It was not a statue. It was a young man in costume. A mime, he realized, one whose job it must be to stand in front of the carousel for hours at a time without moving a muscle, attracting customers.

He stared incredulously at the young mime. "You've been following me."

"You're Madsen, aren't you?"

"What?"

"Sure you are. From *As the World Ends*? It's my favorite show! I've been watching it since I was a little boy."

The mime reached under his jacket and brought out a damp piece of paper and a ball-point pen.

"Would you mind?"

"You've got to be kidding."

The young man blinked through running makeup. The smile faded.

"What's the matter? Too stuck-up to sign autographs for your fans?"

They stood there in the cave, daring each other to back off, as the sea lions barked from the sidelines.

When he finally managed to call from a pay phone, a computerized voice told him that the number he had dialed was no longer in service.

That was impossible. Had it been so long? Only last Christmas he had spoken to them, or was it New Year's? And he had sent his mother something on her birthday, and his father, after the operation. Surely he had done that.

Directory Assistance was unable to help.

Had they taken an unlisted number? That was reasonable, he supposed. Reporters had a way of tracking down relatives for gossipy feature stories; he had learned that the hard way during his first marriage.

He drove out along back streets to the house where he had grown up. The plain stucco one-story had still been his address when he began reading for little theater parts in high school. It was where he had sat up nights memorizing lines in his room, where he had lost his virginity to Carol Moreland while his parents were gone on vacation. After that he had seen them less often as rehearsals kept him away from home except to eat and sleep, until he could afford his own apartment. By his mid-twenties his life-style had become something his parents could no longer share or understand.

As he turned the corner he slowed, wondering if this was the right street, after all. The trees were denser and older, their split limbs hanging low over a buckled sidewalk. The houses seemed small and dingy, with cracked drive-ways and peeling facades. But then he reached the end of the block and recognized the sagging mailbox, the one he had repaired for his dad before moving out.

While maneuvering for a place to park be-tween unfamiliar automobiles, he noticed a sign stuck into the ground at the edge of the property, next to the weathered fence and the oleander bush:

FOR SALE.

It couldn't be true. But the lawn was parched and overrun with weeds, the screen door rust-ing, the bare windows clotted with grime. One of the panes had been broken out and left un-replaced. That was not like his dad. It was not like him at all.

He got out of the car and went to the shat-tered window.

Squinting between the dust and harsh shadows, he saw a torn curtain hanging from a twisted rod, an emptied bookcase. The floor he knew so well was bare, the boards scuffed and warped. Through the kitchen doorway he could make out denuded cupboards and the misaligned geometry of water-damaged linoleum.

He rang the bell at the next house. No one answered there, though when he walked away a pale face withdrew from the front window, as if someone were hiding inside, too frightened of him to open the door.

The post office had no forwarding address.

He was about to give up, when he remembered the real estate company on the sign.

"We don't give out that kind of information," a suspicious woman told him over a cluttered desk.

Don't you recognize me? he thought. Monday through Friday at two o'clock, the most popular show in its time slot? But judging by the mound of papers in front of her, the realtor did not have time to watch afternoon television. Or perhaps she did and mistook him for Madsen, the despicable character he portrayed. Could that be it?

"I'm their son," he explained.

The way he delivered the line he had trouble believing it himself. Even his driver's license would not prove it. He had changed his name years ago.

"Please," he said, allowing his voice to break with a hint of desperation.

"Well," she said, "there *is* a box number. So we can send them the escrow papers. That's all I have. It's the way they wanted it. I'm sorry . . ."

The box number turned out to be a mail drop in Santa Maria that shared space with a parcel delivery service and an instant-printing franchise.

The clerk there was no help. The man refused even to admit that he had a list of names and addresses for those who rented his postal boxes. It was not hard to understand. The one thing such a business had to sell its customers was anonymity.

What else was there to do? He was not ready to quit. It was Saturday and he did not have to be at the studio. He had told Claire he would meet her after the engagement shower tonight, but that was still hours away.

If he did not find them today, what then? A letter? He had come out to tell them the good news in person. They would want to meet his fiancé and her family. There were details to be worked out—the reception, the guest list. He could have his secretary do it all. But his parents deserved to be involved. He owed them that much. He had waited too long already, and the wedding date was closing fast.

"Excuse me," he said again to the man at the counter.

The clerk finished loading a ream of bond paper into the photocopy machine.

"Something else I can do for you?"

"Listen." He felt like a spy attempting to buy secrets behind enemy lines. He took another look at the clerk, the distracted eyes that bulged from the sharp scent of solvent, the ink-stained fingers. "I'll make you an offer. You don't have to tell me anything."

"Right," said the clerk, "I don't."

"All you have to do is take a break." He reached for his wallet. "While you're away, let's say somebody slips behind the counter and gets a peek at your files. By the time you come back I'm gone. You didn't see a thing. How does that sound?"

He took out a twenty and held it casually between two fingers.

"Sounds like you're a cop."

"I'm not."

"Bill collector, then." The clerk's eyes fixed on him. "Are you skip tracing?"

"That's right." He lowered his voice as an old man from the laundromat next door entered and headed for the locked mail compartments, key in hand. He fished out another twenty. "I'm skip tracing. Now can you help me? Or do I get a court order? That would be a lot of trouble. For both of us."

"Then I guess you'll have to get your court order," said the clerk, his back straight, his face steely. "It's hard enough to make a decent living without your kind."

Frustrated, he leaned across the counter. "Okay, I'm not a bill collector. I already told you—I'm looking for my folks. I don't know where they live."

"How come you don't know a thing like that?"

"They moved."

"Sure."

It was no use. He put the money away, defeated.

As he made for the door he passed the old man with the laundry bag, who was fumbling with his letters and relocking his box, one of hundreds of numbered metal compartments set into the wall.

He stopped and faced the clerk again.

"I'll wait, then," he said defiantly. "They have to come in to pick up their mail sooner or later."

The clerk lumbered out from behind the counter. "I don't want you in here. I've seen you before, hanging around."

"You've never seen me in here." You're confused, he thought, like everybody else. I'm not

Madsen. "I'm an actor, for God's sake. It's only a part."

"My son was an actor," said the old man.

He was startled by the voice. He looked at the balding head, the stooped posture, the gray skin. It was difficult to believe that anyone could have changed so much.

"Dad?" he said.

"I wouldn't have recognized you, son."

"Never in a million years," said his mother.

"No?" He forced a laugh. He had grown the beard three or four years ago, for the show. Didn't they remember?

"Does it itch?" asked his father.

"A little. I guess I don't notice it anymore." He cracked his knuckles and sat back in the Winnebago, then leaned forward again. At his spine was his dad's laundry bag, a pillowcase spilling clothes yet to be folded, socks and underwear and shirts.

"Let me move that for you," said his mother.

"It's all right," he said.

"I used to hang everything up before it wrinkled," she explained. "But we can't do that now. The laundromat is seven blocks, and there's never a place for the RV. . . ."

"Don't they let you use the washer and dryer?" He parted the curtains at the back of the motor home's kitchenette, pointing at the apartment complex adjoining the lot where they were parked. "After all, you're paying for this space."

"Oh, we're not renting," said his mother. "You see, the nice couple who manage the building are friends of ours. We don't even have a proper address."

"Retired folks," added his father with a wink. "Like us."

"And there are families with children who need clean clothes every day . . ."

"They can't be that nice," he said. "Jesus, it would be the least they could do."

He saw his mother avert her eyes. I shouldn't have taken the Lord's name in vain, he thought. *Language, young man,* he remembered her saying. He had said much worse when he was a teenager, but those three words from her were always enough; the words, and the catch in her voice, the disappointment. He was filled with regret. He wanted to reach out and take her hands.

He cleared his throat.

"You must be hungry," she said.

"Not really." How ungrateful that must sound. "Unless you are." Then he remembered Claire. "What time's it getting to be?"

"You'll stay?" said his mother.

He checked his watch.

"Let me take you out to dinner," he said.

"Oh, no. The decent places are all so expensive . . ."

"Even with our seniors' discount," his father said.

"Don't worry about it. It's my treat."

"We couldn't let you do that," said his mother. "We know how hard it's been."

"What do you mean? I can afford it."

His mother smiled indulgently.

"Don't you believe me?" he said. "Do you know how much they're paying me every week?"

"You have a regular job, then?"

He almost laughed. "Well, I don't know if you can call it that, but—"

"It's all right," said his father.

"What is?"

He did not understand. Unless they, too, had him confused with the character he played on *As the World Ends*. It was not possible. Was it?

"You don't believe that soap opera, do you?"

Then he saw the portable television set, its antenna poking out between the cardboard cartons above the trundle bed. It was dusty with disuse. He was relieved, until he realized that they did not even know about the show.

"It must have been hard," his father said, "after you and Carol broke up."

His mother leaned closer. "She was never really one of us, you know."

He blinked. "Carol?" The girl he had gone with in high school. "That was—a long time ago."

"You had to find out for yourself," said his father. "I know how it is."

"I could fix something to eat," said his mother.

"Later." I'll go out and pick up some food, he thought. Soon. Time was running out. Like irregular rows of stones, the tops of parked cars cast lengthening shadows across the apartment complex lot; the motor home's shadow was the longest, extending to the side of the building itself, like the adumbration of something long forgotten whose presence remained inescapable. "Just some coffee for now," he said. "If it's not too much trouble."

His mother busied herself with plastic cups and spoons, heating water on the mini-stove. Above the hissing of a propane flame he heard children roaming free in the hallways between the nearby apartments, finding their own reckless way, making choices the consequences of which would not be felt for years to come. When she sat down with the coffee, she had a book under her arm

"I'll bet you don't remember this," she said.

"What?"

Then he recognized the slender volume as his junior high school yearbook.

"Mama, please," he said.

"Just you wait, now . . ."

He braced himself for yet another look at his infamous full-page portrait as class president, the one with his hair slicked back in the geeky style of the times, his fly partially unzipped for all the world and posterity to see.

Instead she flipped to the back of the book and the group photos.

"Here."

Each side of the two-page spread contained a pair of homeroom classes. She tapped one of the wide-angle photographs.

"This one."

His mother beamed.

He scanned the back row of the panorama for his own scrubbed features, centered as always among the tallest in his age group. He did not find it. He checked the caption. Yes, it was his old homeroom, the 7–15's. Had he been absent that day?

"Where?"

She laid a finger near the bottom of the page.

Next to her fingernail was the front row, made up of the shortest students, mostly boys. The heads of the thirteen-year-olds were no larger than buckshot. How ridiculously young they looked, dressed in jeans with rolled cuffs and shirts picked out for them by their mothers, grinning toothlessly as though it all mattered.

"I don't—"

She tapped her finger.

There, at the edge of the first row, one little boy stood apart from the rest. He posed with his thumbs hooked in the pockets of his rumpled, ill-fitting denims, his chin stuck out pugnaciously.

Somehow, in that part of his mind where such things were recorded forever, he seemed to recall a similar T-shirt with faded stripes, the short sleeves too tight . . .

But he had never looked like this. His clothes were always pressed. And by then he had already grown to most of his adult height. That was why he had been chosen for the Drama Club, so that he could play older characters.

"Let me see this," he said.

He riffled to the portraits of class officers, found the right page and pressed it flat.

"There. Remember now, Mom?"

"What is it you want to . . . ? Oh, yes! Wasn't he the nicest young man? I often wonder what became of him. Maybe if you'd had friends like that . . ."

He took the book away from her.

There was the seventh-grade class president, wearing a letterman's sweater and a world-weary smirk. If you looked closely you could detect the unforgettable half-opened zipper.

Only it was not his face.

It was another boy's.

"And this one . . ." his mother said.

She brought out more yearbooks. He recognized the colors of his school, the dates. And yet each told a different story from the one he remembered. A very different story.

"These books," he said. "Where did you get them?"

"I've saved them all," she said. "They're the only record of the past now."

Whose past? According to these he had never been elected class president, had never served on the student council or edited the school newspaper or starred in the senior play. He had never earned the grade point average that kept him at the top of his class.

"How could you be proud of someone like that?"

"We are," said his father.

"But—"

"You're our only son," his mother said softly. "You're all we have."

He paced the short distance of the Winnebago's interior.

"Let me get this straight," he said. "You don't remember the acting scholarship, the trip to New York, the auditions, the jobs? The reviews?" He had sent them copies, hadn't he? "Then Hollywood and the series, the daytime TV?"

"That was always your dream, I know," said his mother. "You would have done those things if you'd had the opportunity. I'm sure of it. I only wish we could have helped you more."

"Then what *do* you remember? When was the last time I came out to see you, for example?"

"At the old house?" His mother's hands fidgeted. "Let's see. It would be just after you and Carol—had that trouble. And you went away. Not that we blame you. She was a worthless piece of fluff."

"What else? What about *your* lives?"

"Well, after your father's operation there wasn't anything left, of course, even with the Medicare, so . . ."

"So we made the best of it," said his dad. "The same as you. That's life."

"You didn't get the checks?" he said. "I told my secretary to mail them out." I did, he thought, I swear.

"You would have if you could," said his mother. "We know that. But now you're here, and that's all that matters. We always knew you'd come back."

"Do you need a place to stay, son? Just till you get on your feet. There's always room for one more."

"A family has to take care of its own," said his mother.

"Or we're no better than animals," said his father.

His legs began to fail him. His head reeled under the low ceiling and his eyes lost focus in the dimness. He groped for the door at his back.

"Excuse me," was all he could say before he staggered outside.

After six rings he gave up. He lowered the phone.

Just before he let go of the receiver there was a faint click on the other end.

"Post-Production."

He fumbled it back up to his ear. "Marty?"

"Talk to me."

He felt a surge of relief. "Marty, thank God."

"Who's this?"

A tingle in the pit of his stomach, like the feeling in the middle of the night that wakes you up before you know why.

"Who do you think?"

A shuffling on the other end, Marty's voice fading in and out. "Listen, we're up to our assholes here, so—"

"Put me through to Jack."

"Jack's not here. Who am I speaking to?"

He was afraid to say his name. What if Marty did not recognize it?

"Debbie, then. She's there, isn't she?"

"Who?"

77

"Debbie Conner." My assistant, he thought. Or at least that's the way I remember it.

"You got the wrong extension. Dial again and—"

"Who's in the booth?"

"Nobody."

"Somebody has to be in the booth! Who's directing?"

"There *is* no director," said Marty. "We don't *need* a director. It's Saturday—we're doing sound cues. Bye."

The phone went dead.

He stood by the pay phone, between Beach Boy's Chinese Food and Sinbad's. To the east, new signs broke the skyline like alien coral. American Diner, Chiporama, Frostie . . . all unrecognizable. When had it happened?

Shaking, he took out another coin.

He could call his agent. Or his accountant. Or his secretary.

But not till Monday morning.

And he could not wait that long.

There was still Claire . . .

But what if she did not know him, either? Was he ready to face that?

Instead he let the receiver slip from his grasp and leafed through the directory.

Marcos, Morehead, Morel . . .

Moreland, Carol.

78

She was in the book, his old girlfriend. And the address was the same. She was still here. She had never moved.

He could call her . . .

When she answered, what would she say? And what would he say to her? That he had come back to make things right? Was that even possible now? What if she remembered a different past, too—what if it really was too late?

His fingers closed and tore the page out.

He walked on, feeling the boards creak and begin to give way beneath his feet.

HELP KEEP YOUR PIER BEAUTIFUL, warned a sign. PLEASE USE RECEPTACLES.

Without breaking stride he dropped the page into the trash can.

My first love, he thought. So many years ago. And all this time I've told myself I was right to end it. That it was good for both of us to move on, following separate paths. I rationalized that there was more. For me. And for her. I thought she left for the city when I did. I told myself that.

But she didn't have the strength.

Or the recklessness.

People should look after each other. Or we're no better than animals.

I did that, didn't I?

No. I went off to find a way, *my* way. Everyone else be damned.

Dennis Etchison

And now the score is evening up. . . .

He raised his collar and continued walking.

The Playland Arcade was still open. Bright lights, people of every age hunkered over the games. Genesis, Big Choice, Party Animal, Battle Zone, Bad Dudes, Banzai Run, Millionaire, Eight Ball, Forgotten Worlds, The Real Ghostbusters.

He stopped to watch them. They were so intent on the play, as balls were lost in the machinery and points accumulated, to be added up or subtracted at the end, depending upon one's control. He considered going inside. Then he noticed a sign at the entrance:

> FAMILY FUN ZONE
> BAD LANGUAGE
> NO   VIOLENCE
> LOITERING

He moved on.

Ahead was the old carousel, closed for the night, and opposite it a large unfinished building: FUTURE HOME OF THE MUSEUM OF MARINE MAMMALS. Farther along, at the tip of the pier, only a bait and tackle shop, and beyond that darkness.

Behind him, the waterfront restaurants and shops and street signs pointing the way into a strange town.

I could go back, he thought. But what's left?
What have I done?

I identified with my role, ignoring everything
else; that was my mistake. If you do that sort of
thing, you become that sort of animal. I was too
lost in the game to realize. And now it has come
due at last, an empty sum with nothing to draw
on. The good eroded by the bad, as if it never
existed.

Only this moment.

That was why they gave us memory. Without
it everything else falls away, the legacy of the
past is trashed and we are left stranded.

The logic is perfect. The future created by the
present, the present by the past . . .

But there is one part they don't tell you.

It works retroactively—in both directions.

Now a rumbling sounded directly beneath
him, as if the earth were about to open.

It was the tide rolling in, clacking the stones,
pounding the boulders and resounding through
each fractal inch of the shoreline.

He held the rail.

Out there, he knew, was the rock where something lived, something old, a species out of
touch with the mainland and all but forgotten.
Were they trapped? Unless someone came to
show the way, they would remain there, cut off,
until they were finally dragged to shore and in-

stalled as curiosities in the marine museum to die.

He wanted to go out there, to be there with them. But the sea was dark, and even the jetty was lost to him now.

A sudden breeze stirred.

He thought he heard a cry drifting in on the waves.

He listened intently, until the cry was no longer distinguishable from any other sound in the night.

Then he shivered as the breeze strafed the pier, swept the boards and returned to the open sea.

The white form of a pelican rose above the breakers and began to circle slowly, its pale wings extended as if anticipating an embrace. As the circle widened to include the pier, it came to rest atop the carousel enclosure.

His eyes followed the line of the roof down to the boardwalk.

Incredibly, the mime was still there. So taken with his role, perhaps, that he was not aware of the hour, unwilling or unable to leave.

You may as well go home now, he thought. It's over.

He walked past, turned and came back, studying the face that was frozen behind a mask of greasepaint.

The mime stared straight ahead, at a spot on

the horizon where the sun had gone down.

"Hi."

The mime did not move a muscle.

He cleared his throat and tried again. "Remember? This afternoon. You called me—something. A name. What was it?"

He moved in, closing the distance between them until their faces were inches apart.

"What did you call me?" he said. "I can't remember."

The mime refused to answer.

"Please. I need to know."

They stood there facing each other. Time passed, each second slipping into the next and lost forever. He waited, but there was no response.

On Call

"Read it now," called the blind newspaper vendor. *"Many are dying and many are dead!"*

Wintner geared down and rounded the corner, trying to spot an opening. He glided past a photo shop, a dry cleaners and laundromat, a stationers, a multi-leveled parking structure that covered half the block and, at the next corner, the florist's stall. He felt a fleeting regret that from this lane he was unable to catch even a glimpse of the young woman who worked there; most days he noticed her on his way back from the freeway, her face moving in among the flowers there, and the cheerfulness of the sight, the very rightness of it, seemed to shorten the distance of his commuting and make his burdens somehow easier to bear. But today was Saturday, anyway, he remembered. He kept going.

He would have to drive round again.

He could, of course, find a parking place easily enough in the municipal structure—but then Laurie never liked having to walk all that way from the clinic entrance.

How long would his wife be this time? Ten minutes? More like twenty, he thought, if she's running true to form. Or thirty. *I only have to find out about the x rays*, she had said. *It won't take long.*

God, he hoped so. He knew what happened to time when her mind got hold of it.

He circled the block once more, just as a black Mustang slid into a vacant space in front of the clinic office. He groaned and set his teeth. He had lost track of how many times he had gone around. He turned his wrist to check his watch, but couldn't remember how long it was since he had dropped her off.

He neared the corner.

Already it was turning late in the day. He noticed now that the buildings had begun to resemble oblong boxes, row upon row of them set on end, as shadows filled the doorways and slanted down from the rooftops. He slowed to a crawl and saw that his car was actually pacing one of the pedestrians, a stoop-shouldered old man who was stepping laboriously along the sidewalk that fronted the clinic. Wintner shuddered without yet understanding why and eased on up the block.

There was a taxi zone at the traffic light. He slipped into neutral and rolled in close to the curb. He cut the ignition, adjusted the rear-view mirror so that he could see her when she came out, and sat listening to the ticking down of the engine as it tried to cool.

A meter maid cruised past his open window. She shook her helmet and motioned for him to move on. He nodded. When she came by a second time—forty minutes later—he started the car and crossed the intersection and drove until he found a place to park on the next block.

"I'm sorry," said the nurse, "but I can't find a *Mrs. Winter*—is that the name? I don't see her down here in the book."

"She only stopped in to find out about her tests." He offered a smile, got a good look at the nurse and withdrew it. "It must have been about an hour ago."

"Well, just a sec. I'll ask the other girl."

Girl, he repeated to himself in wonderment. Only the very young—and the middle-aged, like these—call themselves that. How many more years will they be able to get away with it? Until their faces crack and turn to dust?

Dennis Etchison

Wintner scanned the waiting room. Even, monotonous walls, a reading rack haphazardly stocked with plastic-bound magazines, a planter stuck full of dingy artificial flowers. An endless dose of taped music issued forth from a concealed speaker; reflexively he identified the selection as the theme from the movie *Doctor Zhivago*.

A second nurse appeared from behind the frosted partition.

"Sir?" she said in a precise, controlled tone. Like a librarian, he thought.

She waited for him to approach her.

"Your wife's probably with one of the doctors. He may have wanted to go over the results with her. Why don't you find a seat for a little while longer? I'm sure she'll be out any minute."

There was a cool authority to her voice. It must come with the territory, he thought. Or maybe she had been a librarian once, a long time ago. He could have pressed her, but why bother? She was undoubtedly right. Besides, he was hot and tired and—he let it pass.

He faced the waiting room. No. He shook his head. He certainly did not need to rub shoulders with a roomful of poor, sick bastards, not right now. He avoided looking at them. A permanent rain check on that one, he thought, sighed, and headed back out, past a rosy woman and her two apple-faced children.

The Death Artist

* * *

There was a hofbrau on the other side of the street, barely identifiable by a fringe of old-world lettering. He took a seat at the bar, keeping an eye on the front of the clinic building.

He ordered a schooner of Lowenbrau Dark and stared past the beef jerky and pickled eggs until the stein was empty.

Still no sign of Laurie.

He started on another Lowenbrau and, surprisingly, began to feel the effects. It hit him then: he hadn't taken time yet to eat today. It seemed that he had spent every minute on the run, placing calls, shuffling his schedule so that he would get her here before the clinic closed . . .

As he approached the office, he couldn't help noticing how dirty it really was. The paint appeared to peel off the door even as he reached for it: the stucco was beginning to crumble from around the foundation, falling away into piles of pulverized dust like insect droppings. There was an official-looking notice tacked to the door, something about National Suicide Week. He didn't take time to read it.

A new, younger nurse glanced up. He spread his hands on the counter.

"And how are you feeling today?" she asked. Her eyes flicked over him, reading his features as she reached for a form.

"I feel fine," he began. "It's my wife. I know this sounds crazy but—"

He told her what had happened. When he finished she said, "I'll see."

He watched as another white figure materialized behind the opaque glass. He heard the first nurse recapping the story.

She concluded, "I thought maybe he should see Dr. . . ." He didn't catch the name.

The other nurse, the fourth one he had seen today, looked him up and down. He was beginning to feel like a man caught without papers in a nudist camp.

She moved her head briskly from side to side. He could almost hear a mental *click* as she came to a decision.

"No," she said, "I don't quite think so." Then, to him: "Maybe she's incognito."

"What?"

"I say, she may be incognito, do you think so?"

"That's what I'd say," said the other nurse. "Try that."

"Incognito?" he repeated. He seemed to have missed something. He replayed the word several times in his mind until it lost meaning.

"You could at least check," said the first nurse, returning to her chair, as the senior nurse disappeared behind the partition.

He felt like laughing. He held out his hands

helplessly, turning around to share the joke with anyone who might have been listening.

But no one paid any attention. Actually, he thought, maybe I should have waited here from the very beginning. Maybe I missed her, after all. Who knows?

Shaking his head, he returned to the door. He passed the same woman with the two children. What kind of place is this? he wondered. Those kids don't look like there's anything the matter with them. Plenty of color in their cheeks. What in hell are they doing here?

She was not at the car.

The sky was darkening rapidly. The street took on a grim, vaguely menacing facade as shadows lengthened over the dim, slick edge of curbing below the disturbing asymmetry of the architecture. Old cornices and abutments and rainpipes jutted like broken teeth too close to the glass panes, rendering the buildings awkward, topheavy, ready to topple; each step he took seemed to threaten to pull everything down around him.

He stopped by the hofbrau, trying to get his bearings. He felt like someone waiting for a train, one that might not even stop at this station.

He saw only a few scattered pedestrians out on the pavement. Even the traffic here had thinned until it was nearly invisible, though he was aware of an almost physical wall of sound from another part of the city. He turned toward the windows of the restaurant and squinted inside.

The faces grouped at the bar were old. All of them. It might have been an illusion caused by the unwashed glass, but he didn't think so.

One face in particular was oddly familiar.

Suddenly he was sure. Yes, he had seen the same man in the waiting room, seated calmly with the others, reading a magazine or—no. He had been staring at the floor. Wintner remembered. The people in the room. They had all been staring at the floor. Waiting.

Only it was not quite the same man. Wintner seemed to remember him as younger, healthier.

He caught his own reflection in the coated glass. And took a breath. He was oddly relieved.

His own face, at least, was more or less as he remembered it.

As he crossed the street to the clinic he checked the shops on either side. They were seedy, rundown. Most of them were already closed for the night. Not one was the kind Laurie would have gone into, anyway.

He thought he saw a figure shuffling away from his line of sight. It was the only movement on the sidewalk now. He could not make out who it was. It could have been one of the shopkeepers locking up and heading home, but for a second he almost recognized the gait.

The doorknob practically came off in his hand.

An elderly couple brushed past him on their way out, smelling of lilac and formaldehyde. He could see two new nurses, both younger than the others he had spoken to. As he neared the counter they stopped talking. He almost heard what they were saying.

"Did you have an appointment?" said the first one. She glanced worriedly at the clock which hummed high and white on the wall. "Most of the doctors have gone, I'm afraid."

"Listen," he said, and he began. He told her. Then he said, "I want to talk to whoever's in charge. Then I want her, or you, or someone to check the examination rooms, the offices, the bathrooms, for God's sake. I want to know if my wife's still in this building, and I want to know now."

"Just a moment, sir."

Her fingers tapped the sterile counter.

As he stood there, a door to an inner office swung open and the woman with the two children came out. A nurse held the door for them. They needed it. The woman moved so slowly she seemed at death's door; the children were pale as ghosts.

He nodded automatically as they passed. The

old woman raised her tired eyes, noted his face and muttered something unintelligible.

"This way please."

At first he didn't know the nurse was talking to him. Then he saw that the white door was being held open like a protective wing. For him.
. "You found her," he said, his muscles relaxing.

The nurse cleared her throat but said nothing.

He followed her. The hallway was as immaculate as her starched uniform. He heard the swishing of her white stockings as she led him to a room at the end of the corridor.

"The doctor on call will help you," she said. "Just a—"

She shut the door behind him.

The office was comfortably appointed in leathers and dark woods. There was another door on the other side. He tried an overstuffed chair, but only got up again to pace the carpet. Books were everywhere, and entombed among them within the walls were various artifacts that appeared to be the taxidermied remains of small animals of unknown species.

He went over to the desk.

A sheaf of notes tucked under the border of a thick blotter. An open notebook filled with indecipherable scratchings. Behind the desk, an assortment of framed certificates from foundations around the country, including one from the Menninger Clinic in Topeka.

So that was it. He was a head man—some kind of doctor for the monkeys of the mind.

Is that what they think I need?

He took a step back. His shoulder touched one of the bookcases. He turned.

A row of glass vials sealed in resin, each larger than the last. They contained embalmed extractions of some strangely familiar organisms floating in various stages of growth. His eyes followed the sequence. Near the end of the line the vials became bottles, then jars.

What have they done with her? he thought.

A thump sounded at the far wall, from behind the door to the other side. Without thinking, he closed his fingers around one of the glass specimens.

The door clicked and started to whisper open.

His body jerked as his feet moved backward too fast. He fumbled for the door to the hall, found the knob and stumbled out.

There was a movement behind him but he did not look back. He heard the nurses' crepe soles squeaking across the reception room floor. He heard their nervous, practiced, too young voices, saw their grasping hands in a blur as he ran past. He saw the vinyl curling around the aging magazines, smelled the waft of preserved death in the air. He smelled the chemicals on their skin, felt the cold, smeared door and the sudden rush of night air on his chest. He tasted the darkness and the clot of fear in his throat.

As he ran, voices struggled to be heard within him.

The nurses. What had they been saying when he came in? It had sounded like—like—

We live by death, he thought they had said.

And the newspaper vendor. Wasn't there something more the blind man had been shouting?

None of the dead have been identified, he thought it was.

And the old woman. What had she been trying to tell him?

We are the dead, she had said. *We are the dead*.

He wound down to a fast walk. He could almost see the ancient man who had been shuffling along the sidewalk earlier, away from the clinic. A man who had once, not too long ago, perhaps not too long ago at all been so much more than he was now.

He found himself at the corner, next to the flower stall. It was dark, empty except for the sickly-sweet scented wreaths and arrangements waiting in the shadows.

He shuddered and crossed the street swiftly, mechanically, trying to make it to the car.

He passed the hofbrau.

The faces were inside. They were grouped

around the dark wood bar, all of them old beyond belief now and sick unto death, staring into their glasses, waiting. They reminded him of faces he had seen before.

Then he saw the flower girl.

He pushed his way inside.

She was standing there. Her voice alone was almost cheerful as she began to move among them, asking questions, giving advice, making arrangements. He noticed for the first time that she was armless on one side, her pink stump smooth and rounded under the opening in her summer dress.

How long has she been that way? he wondered. Or does it work the other way for her, too? He thought crazily, *Was she born with even less?*

He stood shivering, watching her animated form and the vase of wilted flowers at the end of the dark, polished bar. After a minute she became aware that she was being watched.

Slowly he held out his hand to her.

"I brought you something," he heard himself saying, still uncertain, trying to think of the right words as he handed her the bottle. "I—I thought you should see it. God damn you."

She turned in painstaking slow motion, her muscles stopping and starting, stopping and starting with each part of the movement, until at last her eyes met his.

Dennis Etchison

"What?" she said.

There was a pause that seemed to go on forever. Then someone offered up a sound that
was somewhere between a laugh and a death-
rattle, and the black fear was on him.

Deadtime Story

His name was Shaun and he worked at the Stop
'N Start Market, the afternoon shift. It was only
thirty hours a week but it would be enough to
pay his first year at Santa Monica College—as
long as he could take living at home, that
is. Somehow he managed to schedule all his
courses before noon, no mean feat in itself; that
left him exactly one hour. He would bolt from
his last class at the bell, skipping lunch in order
to stop by the campus library, then hoof it down
Pico to Twenty-sixth Street, where he had to
change clothes and be ready for the counter at
one o'clock sharp. Raphe needed all the help he
could get ringing up the Twinkies and Monster
Slurps and microwave burritos before the rush

was over, and as long as Shaun clocked in on time and made sure that what he put in the safe matched the register tape the job was his. He couldn't afford to blow it, even if the pay was only two bits over minimum wage. Where else could he hope to land a job this close to the junior college?

Today the noon crowd was no better or worse than ever, with the usual crush of school kids dodging petty businessmen in the parking lot, littering the tarmac with beef jerky wrappers and half-empty potato chip bags that crunched under the tires of parking cars like sacks of small bones. Inside he recognized a girl from his freshman English class, about to pay for an avocado-and-sprout sandwich and a can of Tab. He ducked into the storeroom and put on his uniform; by the time he came out she was gone. He was relieved not to have to face her in his cap and smock.

"No more calls on Company time," Raphe told him right off.

"Sure, I know that," said Shaun, snapping open a bag big enough to hold the string cheese and six-pack of Olde English 800 on the counter. "I never use the store phone. When do I have time? Hi, Raphe."

"Six ninety-one," Raphe said to the surfer waiting in line. Then to Shaun, "You better tell your buddies to cool it. This one, he kept ringin' all morning. The District Rep was even here. It was embarrassin'. We got work t' do, kid, you know?"

"I know." *He*, thought Shaun, and got a funny feeling. He tried to ignore it. "Did they say who it was?"

Raphe rang up a carton of menthol lights and a Playgirl for the next customer, a long-necked accountant from across the street. "No message. If there was I couldn't make it out. Bad connection. But he wouldn't give up."

"Well, he'll call back, I guess, if it was important." *Don't*, Shaun thought, *please don't* . . .

"He better not," said the manager. "You tell him it's Company policy. No personal calls."

"You got it."

By two o'clock the line had thinned out. It would be awhile before the first afterschool wave came rolling in, piling up bikes and skateboards at the entrance. Raphe doffed his red-white-and-blue cap and started counting down the drawer for a last cash drop before heading out.

For the moment there was no one else in the store. Shaun took a bottle of sparkling apple juice out of the case and one of Mrs. Chippie's oversized cookies from the jar on the counter, adding the exact change to the drawer before Raphe finished with the bills. As he ate, the boy leaned against the newsrack and idly straightened the stacks of stroke magazines and cheap horror novels with metallic cut-out covers. He never bothered to read the books anymore. They were always the same, about possessed children or possessed houses, one or the other, sometimes both. Who had time to worry about stuff like that? He tipped the bottle back and drained it. This was the first break he'd had all day and the apple juice tasted like gold.

"Hey, Raphe?"

"Ninety-three, ninety-four, ninety-five . . ."

"I was wondering."

"Ninety-eight, ninety-nine, a hundred bucks. Yeah?"

"What'd be my chances for getting in some overtime?"

Raphe frowned. "You seen the rubber bands?"

"Next to the *TV Guide*s."

"What do you mean, overtime?"

"Well, I was just thinking. I'm finished with my midterms, and Easter's coming up. I could use the extra money."

"I got Craig down for seven-to-midnight. He never misses, you know that. He needs the money, too."

"I know. But what about the late shift? I could do Fridays easy. No classes on Saturday, so I could sleep in. Unless you already have somebody regular."

Raphe paused with the bundle of bills, staring out at the grey pavement and the battered cars rippling past on the other side of the glass, the mix of faceless strangers jerking along the dirty sidewalk. He raised an eyebrow tiredly.

"How old are you now, kid?"

"Sev—" Shaun caught himself in time. "Eighteen. So?"

"So you don't want the late shift," said Raphe. "The kind that come in here then, they belong in a zoo. Take my word for it. Plus there's always holdups. I don't wanna lose you that way, boy. You need the money that bad, get it from your folks."

"Well, see, I can't do that. They don't even want me in school. My old lady's divorced. She thinks I should go to work full-time."

"You got the rest of your life to worry about full-time. Take my advice. Don't drop out. You still got a chance." He deposited the wad of bills, reset the time lock on the safe. "You forgot something."

"I did?"

Raphe reached into the drawer, took out a dollar and some change and slid it across the countertop, then made it up from his own pocket.

"What's that for?"

"Don't worry about it. The Company can afford to buy you lunch once in a while. Those guys they give me for the late shift, if you knew what they get paid . . . I don't know where they come from. Wetbacks or somethin'." He stopped before he said too much. "Anyway, this time it's on the house."

"Aw, no, man, I can—"

"Don't argue. It's Stop 'N Start policy." Raphe made his way back to the storeroom. "See you tomorrow, kid. And if Greg is late, I want to know. Got that?"

"Yeah, sure, Raphe. And thanks. I really—"

The phone rang.

Shaun waited for Raphe to pick it up. But the manager was all the way in the back room. What if it was the main office? Raphe would want to know. The boy hesitated, then answered.

"Hello?"

"Hello, who is this?"

He fell back into his role. "Stop 'N Start, We Never Sleep. May I help you?"

"Well, I'll be gonged. I finally got a live one." A chuckle. "And I even recognize your voice."

The line swirled away in a static wind, as if the call were coming from a long way off, then reformed. Now the voice on the other end was close again, the tone so intimate that Shaun's ear twitched as though it had been touched by lips he did not know. He held the receiver an inch away from his face. "You do?"

"Sure. Did you think we forgot?"

Shaun felt a grabbing in his spine. He couldn't shake it off.

"Sorry, but I'm really busy right now. If there's nothing I can—"

"We never forget. We don't like to lose track of our own. You had us lookin' in all the wrong places. What did you have to go and do that for? But I wanted to let you know. *It won't be long now.*"

Shaun ducked down and pretended to re-stock the cigarettes, taking the phone with him. "Listen, I can't talk. I've got a customer." It was true; he heard the blue dinging of the electric eye at the door. "Besides, you have the wrong person. If this is some kind of joke . . ."

"Joke?" A chuckle. "Is that all it means to you?"

"I don't know what you're talking about."

"Don't you? Well, you didn't think it was a joke that night. Or have you forgotten that, too?"

Shaun peered out between the disposable lighters and the display of Hostess Cupcakes and Mickey Banana Dreams. Suddenly he realized that he had not forgotten, after all. That bored night at the Club, looking for something, anything to give the edge back to his life; the ones he had met there, the beers outside, then the game, and the promises—the pact. In the morning it had seemed like a bad dream. He had hoped it would go away. But now he knew that it would not. He hadn't forgotten. And neither had they. The refrigerated cases were cool and still, with no movement reflected in the misty glass doors. Had someone come in or not?

"What do you want from me?" he said.

"Nothing that you don't want to give. A guy's only as good as his word. And I always keep mine."

As Shaun stood up he almost lost his balance. His temples throbbed, his kidneys ached, like that afternoon in the seventh grade when he had gone out to fight Billy Black at the edge of the park after school. All that day he had tried not to think about it. But when it was finally time there was nowhere to run. He had wobbled then, too, going out to meet it.

"*When?*" he said into the mouthpiece.

"Hey, I can't tell you that, now, can I? It would spoil everything."

The line broke again, crackling like cellophane peeled off a pack of cigarettes. Then it steadied and cleared, so near that it might have been coming from inside his own skull.

"Where are you?" said Shaun. "At least tell me that much."

"Close, Shaunie. Closer than you think."

The there was only the chuckling.

The boy slammed down the phone, missed the cradle the first time, fumbled it back into place. He stood. The seals on the cold cases must have been leaking. The air inside the store was suddenly so chilly that he could hardly breathe.

He leaned out into the aisle. "Can I help you? Is anybody—hello? Is anybody there?"

The long, jagged rows of packaged goods fanned out before him. He couldn't see into more than one row at a time.

There was a rumbling.

He turned. In the parking lot outside, a spotted Chevy Malibu circled the store and dipped out into traffic. Raphe's car.

The manager had walked right by while he was on the phone. He hadn't yelled. He hadn't said anything. Shaun saw him now through the window, hunched resignedly behind the wheel, taking his leave as quietly as a father who has been betrayed by one of his own children. Sorry, Raphe, he thought. It won't happen again, you'll see. The next time that white-haired son of a bitch calls I'll tell him to—

Tell him what?

Give me one more chance, thought Shaun. *They've got to. Oh God, please . . . !*

"Shit," he said to the empty rows, the echoing

store. "I really don't fucking *need* this kind of shit right now, you know?"

He stood there stiffly, one hand on the bundle of *Penthouse Variations,* the new April issue with the girl in the mask and leather bondage suit on the cover, and the fingers of his other hand wrapped around the axe handle on the shelf below the counter, waiting to see who would come into the store next.

At a quarter past seven he caught his regular blue bus eastbound on Pico. As he climbed up, the driver pretended not to know him, as usual. Then the driver said, "Hey there, Willy! What you got for me tonight?"

Shaun glanced back at the stepwell and saw a pale man hauling a plastic trash bag onboard. A white hand wriggled out of a dirty coat sleeve, reached into the bag and came up with three oranges.

"Well now, Willy, I don't know. That'll get you to Rimpau, but if you want your transfer . . ."

The pale hand felt around under the coat and emerged dangling a Lady Timex wristwatch.

"Good! That's right, you did good." The driver took the watch and laid it out on the dashboard, next to a box of Bic pens, a brand-new pair of men's deodorant socks, a Mexican wrestling magazine, an Atra razor with the price tag still attached, and a copy of a book entitled *How to*

Profit from Armageddon. "For that, you can ride anywhere you want. Go on an' sit down. Your friends are here already."

Shaun stepped aside. The pale man shuffled to the back and sat between a shopping bag lady and a young man with no eyebrows.

They were all here, the derelicts, the misfits, the outpatients from the VA hospital who had spent the day at the beach and were now returning to voluntary lockup for the night. They were always the first on at Ocean Avenue, filling up the seats in back as the sun turned bloodshot beyond the end of the pier; the Chicana maids and undocumented restaurant workers boarded farther along the route, next to gremmies with skateboards, students on their way to Westwood, pensioners with senior citizen passes, and even the occasional businessman or teacher whose car had broken down one time too many. Until he could afford wheels of his own Shaun was forced to ride this last daylight run with them; the Whammo Express, he called it. Again he wondered where some of the ones in back went after dark, what they would do to shelter themselves if they ever missed the final buses from the beach before the fog rolled in. Sometimes he could imagine himself burning out and turning into one of them like so many other kids he saw, and at such times he was almost glad to have the job and school to keep

him busy. With a shudder he dropped a token
in the fare fox and tried to locate an aisle seat.

Tonight the charity cases took up more space
than usual, occupying at least a third of the vehicle and forcing the paying passengers forward
into every available spot. They're multiplying,
he thought. Like coathangers. Like the garbage
on the streets. Nobody pays any attention, that's
why. And nobody will till it's too late and there's
no room for anybody else. Then what?

He found a place next to two dwarfs wearing
identical polyester leisure suits and too much
aftershave lotion. The twins smiled sweetly at
him as he wedged in on the edge of the seat.
Across the aisle an old soldier stared straight
ahead as the light changed and the bus moved
out.

Shaun gripped his knees and tried not to
think of anything but the patterns of color
sweeping by outside. Fuzzy neon signs were
coming on everywhere, bright lettering and
beckoning doorways and unreadable billboards, swollen tubs of fast food thrust skyward
like offerings to unseen gods, and through it all
the moving crowds, heads down and faces hidden. The bus passed a group of curiosity-
seekers knotted around a dark elongated shape
at the curb. The boy tensed and braced his back
against the seat. It could be any one of them, he
thought, as the bus slowed at the intersection.

He could get on at any time, without warning. Would I even notice him before he works his way back to me and—but the bus driver shifted and rolled past the corner without stopping.

The old soldier began mumbling into a CB microphone. Shaun noticed that the cord dangled in the aisle, unattached.

"Passing Thirty-third Street. Green light. Counted fourteen telephone poles. I forget how many more. Do you have that information? Over."

The boy drew inward, squeezing his hands between his legs. At least this part of the trip was short. If he could make it through the next few minutes he'd be halfway home. Next to him the dwarfs whispered and giggled. He shut his eyes.

Something touched him on the shoulder.

Closer than you think, he remembered, and jumped forward to get away.

A hand pressed him back into the seat. Behind him, a voice spoke directly into his ear.

"Which one?"

He freed himself and half-turned. A male human of indeterminable age was leaning over him, breathing hotly.

"Come on, which one do you want?"

Shaun watched a creased and worn slip of paper unfolded by blackened fingernails.

"My name's Logus. What's yours?"

"Excuse me," said Shaun, "But I have to get off at . . ."

"How about 'Anti-Matter: Does It Matter?' Or 'Heat Death of the Universe.' You look like the type of person who can appreciate that one. Are you a scientist, too? You look like a scientist."

". . . The next stop," said Shaun. The dwarfs were watching him. He scanned the interior of the bus. There was nowhere else to sit.

"Got ten of 'em. Take your pick. Each idea is guaranteed to make you a million dollars. I don't have time myself. Too busy. Right now I'm studying the Heisenberg Principle. Do you know what a Klein bottle is?"

The bus lurched over railroad tracks. Shaun looked out and saw a Polynesian bar, weathered tiki heads guarding the front like relics from a lost civilization, and then the illuminated ideographs of Chinese and Japanese restaurants. Farther on, the marquee of a movie theater and the bloated tenpin sign of the Picwood Bowl, nakedly white and ready to be knocked down. He grasped the back of the seat in front of him and stood.

"Wait," said the voice. "I've got eight more. How about 'White Holes'? That's a good one. You can give me a down payment. I trust you. No checks, though. You'll make a million dollars, I personally guarantee it!"

Even though a shadowy clot of bodies already

waited at the next corner, Shaun yanked the cord. The bus braked with a sound like chalk on a blackboard and they started to force their way in. He saw them pressing on board, eyes averted so that he could not read their faces. Without waiting he swung across the aisle and out the rear exit.

He hoped the connecting bus would not be late tonight. He didn't have his schedule—with a deadening feeling he realized that he had left his book bag. Where? Back at the library, maybe, or at the store. Or on the bus. He couldn't remember. He pictured the dwarfs' small hands pawing through his personal effects. But there was no time to worry about that now. Where was the #8?

He stood apart from the crowd and looked south down the dark tunnel of Westwood Boulevard for a sign. But the approaching headlights were all too small and too low. One set caught him full in the face, blinding him momentarily as it yawed around the corner, spotlighting him as clearly as a jackrabbit on a mountain road. He stepped back. But the side of the building offered little protection.

He could join the others at the bench, try to blend in. . . . Who were they? He couldn't be sure. Their faces were concealed behind turned-up collars. One, a drive-thru cook from the Weenie Wigwam, was munching on a barbecued pork rind. The smell of it blew on the wind. Shaun started to gag.

A dumpy, tattered woman waddled over. Shaun turned away, trying to penetrate the approaching headlights.

"Have you read *The Way of the Wach*?" she said, her voice already rising to a harangue. "It'll help you get a new job. Do you need a raise?"

Shaun ignored her.

"Well sir, you'll get it. Here, read this. It'll help you. Yes, it will. There's always room for one more at the cross!"

He refused the book and hurried across the intersection. He didn't need any of it. He didn't even need the bus. He hadn't remembered to ask for a transfer. But it was just as well. He could walk for now. Besides, this way he would be able to make one more stop. If he dared. What other options did he have? It might be the only chance he would have to make things right. If it was not already too late.

It wasn't far.

The gas station on the corner fired a volley of soft bells at him as cars wheeled past the pumps, their lights wavering coronas through a descending mist. At the Apple Pan customers were lined up three deep behind the stools for pie and hot coffee. He smelled the warmth blowing out the open door as he passed, thought of eating but knew he wouldn't be able to hold it down, not now. He cut left at the first side street and pressed north through a residential neighborhood, moving away from the open boulevard and the traffic.

He crossed Olympic, then the tracks at Santa Monica Boulevard, moving up Glendon so fast that his ankles began to hurt. As he drew closer he felt less protected than ever despite the darkness, with the Mormon Temple to his right as brightly lighted as a movie set, its golden angel with trumpet raised as if to announce his passage. By the time he hit the alley behind the Club he could no longer be sure that he was not being followed.

There were only a few cars behind the building at this hour, making him even more conspicuous as he crunched over gravel to the rear entrance. But at least it wouldn't be crowded inside. They would hear what he had to say. He opened the door beneath the circular sign, the one that was like a clock face with permanently frozen hands, and forced himself to go in.

It was so early that there were only three or four college couples slumming against one wall; otherwise the room was empty except for Big Vivian and a solitary waitress who sat smoking a cigarette. The turntable in the corner was unattended. There was not even a bouncer at the door to collect admission.

The one with white hair wasn't here yet, either.

Vivian was drying soft drink glasses and setting them out behind the bar with anal-retentive determination.

"Any table," she said without looking up. "The music don't start till nine o'clock. You got ID?"

"I'm not here for the music."

"You got to have ID."

"I don't want to stay. I only came by to talk to . . ."

For the first time it occurred to him that he did not know the name of the person he had come here to see. He knew only the image: the hair, the clothes, the voice. The face was unclear in his memory, if he had ever gotten a close look at it. Or had he blocked it out of his mind along with the rest?

"You remember me, don't you?"

"I don't remember nobody," said the owner. "Four dollars."

"I don't want to go down," he said pointing at the fire door. "I just want to talk to—to him. It's important."

"Still cost you four dollars."

"You don't understand. I have to talk to him. *I have to*."

The big woman pressed a button. A red light bulb went on. A bald bouncer came out of the hall, picking his teeth.

Shaun hooked his fingers over the bartop and hauled himself closer.

"Look," he said, "this is private. It's a matter of—" *life and death*, he thought, but couldn't say it. "It's between him and me. Are you gonna let me talk to him or not?"

"Who?"

"You know who I mean."

The bouncer started over.

"Ain't nobody here yet." The big woman reamed out another glass with her towel and eyed the boy. She sized him up, then waved the bouncer off. "Go on home, come back later when—"

"I can't. Don't you get it? I have to talk to him first. I—I have to tell him something."

He couldn't give up. He considered rushing the fire door. But the bouncer had moved over, blocking the way. It was too late. It had always been too late.

"Give him a message, then. Can you do that for me?"

The woman stared him down.

"Tell him it's off. The whole thing. Here." He grabbed a cocktail napkin, started to scrawl a note with his felt-tip highlighter, the only pen he could find. But the letters came out faint and the napkin was wet; the ghostly letters bled and ran together. "Tell him Shaun was here. S-H-A-

U-N. Say that I changed my mind. Do you un-derstand? *Please?"*

She nodded in a way that might have meant anything. One thing was clear. He had been dis-missed. She did not look at him again as she returned to her fragile, spotless glasses.

He left the room exactly as he had found it. Nothing was changed. The couples against the wall were sipping something green and flirting with each others' dates as if there was all the time in the world. Maybe there was, for them. They did not notice him leave. Nobody did. He might not have come in at all.

A fine mist had settled in the lot, coating the stones with slime and turning the trees into gi-ant mushrooms grown up out of the ground while he was inside. At the end of the alley the mist thickened into a fog, masking the traffic that passed on the boulevard as if it did not ex-ist. A distant stoplight blinked its warning at him, winking like a red eye behind spun glass.

Anyone could be out there, waiting. The fog-bound street was white as an ice gauntlet, a gla-cial tunnel where nothing would survive except the most primitive elements. How was he going to get home now? The bus would never see him standing at the corner, and it only ran to Sunset and Beverly Glen anyway. He would still have to walk up the canyon. Even tonight.

He could call somebody.

But who? Who did he know with a car who would come out and get him on a night like this? He gave up on that line of thought. If he had any real friends he would never have gone near the Club the first time.

His mother? No way. She would be dead drunk in front of the TV, as usual. And God only knew where his father was.

What do people in the movies do at a time like this? he wondered.

They . . . they take a cab.

Yes!

He opened his wallet and rifled it for his emergency ten dollar bill. *Be there*, he thought. But it wasn't. He had had to spend it on a book for class yesterday. And he didn't get paid again until Friday.

Now I really am up shit creek, he thought. I am totally, royally screwed.

He felt deep down in his pockets. A couple of dollars worth of change, some bus tokens. How far would that get him? Not far enough. Unless—

There might be a way.

It wasn't much, but it was the only way he could think of. He had never done anything like it before. But it was worth a try.

He couldn't see but he made himself keep going through the fog until he hit the car wash a block down. He didn't look to his right or left but keep walking, watching his tennis shoes and the suction-cup prints they made on the cement. He practically bumped into the phone booth. It was where he remembered it. He rattled the door shut and started leafing through the directory.

The yellow pages were soggy and smelled like laundry that has been left in the washing machine too long. Half of the page he was looking for had been ripped out. The only listing he could read was for the Beverly Hills Cab Company.

He kept slugging in cold coins and dialing until he got through.

It took the cab thirty-five minutes to find him there behind the booth, out of sight of the other cars that whispered past like U-boats on patrol. He only showed himself when he saw the yellow beacon on top. As soon as he got in he locked the door, then told the driver to take him up North Beverly Glen.

The cabby didn't try to fake conversation, which made it easier. Shaun wasn't sure what his own voice would sound like now; it was hard enough to get out the name of the street without stuttering. Judging by the unpronounceable name on the operator's permit, the driver probably did not know more than enough English to get by, anyway.

For the moment the boy was relieved. It

seemed so much safer this way, with the windows rolled up and the heater on, the milky colors of a fogged-in Westwood slipping by on the other side of the glass like a faded mural from a circus sideshow. The driver lowered the volume on his squawk box and didn't ask any questions, whipping around corners as if shortcutting a maze he knew by heart. Shaun couldn't get a clear shot of his face in the mirror, but he didn't care. He only wanted to be home.

Not until they had turned up the Glen and were swinging past the market, tires howling, did he remember what he had to do.

"You tell me where, yes?" said the driver.

"Uh, yeah," said Shaun.

He counted the curves as they pressed higher into the canyon, the few weak streetlights streaking past like melting stars, the untrimmed branches of wild oaks and elms clawing at the car doors. He let the driver pass Chrysanthemum Lane, ready to speak up only when the Café Four Oaks came into view. The signals at Beverly Glen Place would be set on rest-in-red so he knew they had to come to a stop.

"Take a left here," Shaun told him.

"Here?" The turn forked away in three directions, each as dark as a mine shaft.

"Here. See the sign? My house is—is over on Scenario Lane. The one with the porchlight." It was the neighborhood rec center, a converted private residence, but the driver wouldn't know the difference. "Yeah, that one."

The meter totaled as much as Shaun made in three hours at the Stop 'N Start. He got out right away and went into a routine with the wallet. He held the billfold open in front of his face and pretended to count.

"Wow," he said, "I thought I had more than that."

The driver cleared his throat.

"Look, I'll go in the house and get the rest of the money. It's in my other pants. I'll be right back, okay?"

The CB speaker came on again with muffled directions to a long-distance fare. The driver checked his watch. Then he leaned his head out and took a good look at Shaun.

"Can't wait very much long. Right?"

"Right." Shaun flashed a phony smile that still had enough of the old high school charm left to do the trick.

Nod, stuff the wallet in your back pocket and start walking like you know where you're going, he told himself. He felt the headlights on his back as he took out his keys and disappeared around the side of the small house. Immediately he cut across the lot and through the next yard. Presently the sound of the idling taxi was only one more cricket in the night.

He didn't like stiffing the guy, but what else could he do? He would worry about it later, inside. He could mail him the money. Yeah, sure, address it to the cab company with the driver's name, if he could remember it. A weird name, not from anywhere around here. African or Asian or something like that. They would know who he meant.

After a while the cabby started in with his honking, then packed it in when somebody opened a bedroom window and made an impossible anatomical suggestion. A minute later Shaun heard the car gun through a U-turn and roar back down the canyon, radials screaming.

His heart finally began to slow down.

He came out onto the lane and backtracked to the signal. All he had to do now was make a right onto Beverly Glen and walk about two hundred feet and he'd be home. He smiled, relaxing. The paranoia he had felt earlier dissipated with his breath on the air as he smelled the night-blooming jasmine, felt the familiar cracks in the sidewalk under his rubber soles, the same sidewalk he had run up and down so many times as a kid, the sidewalk that never failed to lead him to his house and his room and all the things that kept him safe.

He came to the sign at the corner, the one with the cartoon of a burglar inside a circle with a diagonal line across it and the words

WARNING: THIS AREA PATROLLED BY
NEIGHBORHOOD WATCH. That made him
feel a little bit better. Even the traffic light
showed him a reassuring yellow glow. Suddenly
he wanted to run the rest of the way, through
the café lot and around the last curve, no longer
motivated by fear but eager to be home so that
he could put everything that had happened behind him.

He started down Beverly Glen Boulevard, silent and empty of traffic, the foggy tops of the
peach trees and Chinese plums blurry as Christmas firs draped with angel hair.

And stopped.

There, in the restaurant patio, next to the
Four Oaks sign, was a tall figure.

"Huh," he said to himself, remembering that
it was nothing more than the stunted remnant
of the massive oak that gave the café its name.
It had spooked him more than once as a child.
But not anymore.

Just the same he walked rather than ran, stepping lightly so as not to make too much noise,
reminding himself all the way how foolish he
was being. He tried to see it for what it was. A
game, nothing more serious than those Hallow-
een ghost stories he used to tease himself with,
the shiver that was only fun when it got out of
control. But there was no time for any of that
from now on. There was nothing in the dark

that didn't show. He knew that, he knew it was true.

He tightrope-walked the curb, whistling in the dark, a few bars of "Missing You." He had almost made it to the fence when he heard the song completed for him by a whistling that was not his own.

It was an echo, yes, that was it, the way sounds bounced off the hill behind the reservoir, especially with the canyon so quiet right now, and the fog—

No way.

The tree was still there in the patio. It hadn't moved.

"Hi, Shaunie!"

"Who's there?" he said, backing off the curb.

"It's only me," said the voice. And giggled.

He looked back as the tree changed shape through the fog, crossing the patio, coming this way.

He needed to get past the fence. Then there would only be another hundred feet to go. He could make it in seconds.

"Shaunie," said the voice again. It was small, girlish. It was coming from the other side.

"Melissa? Is that you?"

Yes, he knew that voice. It was the little girl from next door. She wouldn't leave him alone. She and her friends. The tree was in the patio, after all.

Dennis Etchison

"God damn it, Melissa, where are you? Get out here where I can see you!"

"We can't come out, Shaun. We're in our nighties." More giggling. "We're having a slumber party. Do you want to come?"

"Stacey? Jennifer?" He tried to remember the rest of their names. "Go back to bed, all of you. Stop bugging people. Don't you have anything better to do?"

"No."

A head appeared at the top of the fence, freckled and supported by folded elbows.

"Stacey has something to tell you. Don't you, Stace?" Melissa was jerked from below as if by an angry dog. "Cut it out, you guys! What are you, a bunch of queers? Sorry, Shaun, but some people around here are very immature. Anyway, Stacey? she likes you."

"I do not!" said a horrified voice.

"Never mind her. She lies like a rug." Melissa's face seemed to hover disembodied, angelic in the floating mist. "Anyway, we're going in the hot tub later. Do you want to come over?"

"Why don't you pick on somebody your own size?" he told her.

"I'm thirteen."

"You're eleven."

"Well, I'm almost twelve. I got a new bathing suit, a two piece. Don't you want to see it?"

"Good night, little girl. Your mother's calling you."

"Fuck you, Shaun!"

"You wish. Now go back to bed where you belong, like a good kid."

He walked away.

"Melissa's the one who likes you!" a voice called after him. "She says you're cute! She wants to—"

"I do not!"

He heard them squabbling like cats. Kids, he thought. That Melissa . . . maybe in three our four more years. But not now. No way.

He rounded the last stretch, saw the lot full of weeds, his mailbox leaning precariously by the driveway, the relentless growth of bamboo blocking any view of the house from the street. The growth was so dense that it formed a solid barrier; no one passing by would have any idea that a house was there unless they knew where he lived. That was the way his mother wanted it. And tonight he didn't mind.

As he crossed the driveway, dry leaves broke underfoot. He kicked to shake them off.

But there were no leaves in his driveway.

He hesitated at the bottom of the stone steps, listening. The fog blew, moving patches of light and darkness across the glen, the vacant lot, the hillside behind the bamboo, just as it had back in the patio. He was being followed, all right—

by smoke ghosts. Nothing more than that. The sound of leaves? That would be the raccoons coming down to forage under cover of nightfall. He heard them all the time. He had always heard them. So what?

The fog drifted, leaving a patch of white so clear against the dark that it looked like a human figure at the top of the steps. He waited for the shape to blow on.

It did not.

"Mom? What are you doing out here? You'll catch cold. What's the matter? I'm all right. Sorry I'm late. Mom?"

No answer.

It was the kids again, then. One of them. It had to be Melissa. He could tell by the long lines of the nightgown, solid white in the darkness.

"All right, who told you you could come over here? I'm tired. I don't have time for your games. Didn't anyone ever tell you about private property? If you don't go home right now I'll— Melissa? Do you hear me?"

"Shaunie?"

The voice was not high-pitched this time. Not at all.

A car sped around the bend, its tires making a tearing sound. Headlights swept the driveway and the wall of bamboo with twin high-beams, cushioned by the fog but bright enough to outline something at the top of the steps. Then the car was gone. But not before Shaun had time to see what was there, what was really there.

A tall figure dressed in white, arms outstretched.

As Shaun gaped, unable to move, the figure raised a forefinger and made a cutting motion across its throat.

Then it smiled, eyes flashing with a light of their own that shone coldly down the steps and over the boy's startled but unsurprised face, freezing him where he stood.

Later, when the moon was high, the fog continued to hang over Beverly Glen like a shroud.

It remained especially thick in one backyard where, behind a fence, new vapor was rising in a circular cloud.

The little girls had come out to play.

Just now a hand, a very small hand, was reaching out of the misty streamers, feeling for the valve that would release more steaming water into the hot tub from the column of pressure that the girls believed ran all the way to the center of the earth. But the valve would not budge; it was so corroded with mineral deposits that it required more strength to turn than Melissa had in both of her hands.

"Leave it go, Melissa."

"It's not hot enough."

Dennis Etchison

"It *is*. It's a hundred-and-five-degrees, that's what the dial says. Melissa!"

Melissa's hand disappeared as she drifted backward through the warm current. It was almost cool at the surface and yet too hot deep down, though tonight not one of the girls had yet dared to touch bottom. They had changed into their bathing suits and slipped in as quietly as possible, staying close to the edge.

And now the vapor parted as Melissa moved through it, allowing a brief glimpse of the lightly rippled surface. A bubble formed and floated out of sight; they heard it pop in the darkness. Then the steam closed over and there were only the sounds: distant traffic and the clicking of squirrels in the trees, a deep gurgling and, if you listened very closely, a steady hissing that seemed to be near and far away at the same time.

"Is he coming, do you think?" (The voice of Dawn, the ten-year-old.)

"Is who?"

"You know. Shaun."

Melissa sighed, or was it only the hissing? "Whose toe is that? Stay on your own side, will you?"

An acorn fell and struck the ground nearby as the mist drifted unexpectedly, revealing the face of the moon and their thin arms floating on the water. Here a kneecap that was round and white as a cup of snow broke the surface, bobbed and resubmerged; there strings of wet hair flowed out at the waterline around a skinny neck and open mouth.

"He is, I think. I feel like somebody's already watching us."

"Shh," said Melissa, "you want my mom to hear? We're supposed to be asleep, remember? If she finds out we won't ever get another sleep-over." Her hand made a nervous figure-eight in the water.

"I don't care if he comes or not," said Stacey. She arched and floated, paddling in a slow semi-circle. "He thinks he's so big."

"I know you do," said Melissa.

"Stacey doesn't mean that," said Jennifer. "She's just having one of her moods."

"Yeah, her stuck-up mood," said Dawn.

"Her mood of getting a period," said Melissa.

They tried to stifle the giggles. A stream of noisy bubbles blew from their mouths.

Melissa said, "Who got out?"

There was the sound of bare feet slapping on the deck.

"Shh! Did you hear that? If my mom—"

The slapping came closer.

The four girls dunked underwater.

After a few seconds a head ventured up, wet hair clinging. The slapping had stopped.

One by one the others came up for air. Melissa pinched her nose to clear it, still holding her body in to the chin as if hiding under a bedsheet. She looked around as the circles of hair on the water drew upward like flowers closing. She listened, then laughed.

"My gosh," she said, "it's only my baby sister!"

"How did she get out?"

"She's lonesome for me. Aren't you, baby?"

"She's afraid the Lost Ones are gonna get her!"

"There's no such thing," Melissa said. She caught the pudgy two-year-old and swung her over the lip of the hot tub.

"Well hi, baby," said Jennifer in that special singsong voice small girls reserve for dolls and smaller children. She and Dawn and Stacey coasted over to Melissa's side. "Where did she come from? She's getting so big!"

"She's so pretty," said Michelle.

"Have you been bad, Farrah?" asked Dawn. "Have you?"

Baby Farrah started to whimper.

Melissa lifted and coddled her. "I think my sister came out for a swimming lesson."

"Can I hold her? Please?"

"Maybe we'll let you and maybe we won't. Isn't that right, baby? If nobody pokes us with their toes."

"I never touched anybody," said Dawn.

"Me neither," said Jennifer.

"Well, don't look at me, you guys," said Stacey.

"Sure, I really believe that." Melissa shivered and lifted her sister all the way in. With a practiced move she skinned the training panties from her sister's legs. The elastic snapped, shooting away into darkness. "I'll dry you off after and Mom'll never know. Okay?" Cradling the baby, she moved to the center. She dunked several times. Her teeth chattered. "I said s-s-stop kicking me, Stacey!"

"I'm *not*."

Melissa drifted to Stacey's side and reached around the baby's body for the valve.

"But it's hot enough al—"

"Is not," said Melissa. "Anyway, it's my tub. I have to make it hot enough for my sister. Then I'll turn on the Jacuzzi. Help me, somebody, will you?"

Stacey added her hands to the wheel. They buoyed together, tugging until it began to move. Then Melissa found the whirlpool switch.

A hiss of tiny bubbles clouded the water.

From across the yard, the sound of the back door opening.

"Quiet," said Melissa, "it's my mom!"

They waited for the door to slam.

Melissa waved in the thickening steam, motioning everyone down. Three heads plopped out of sight. She kissed her sister, took her deepest breath and ducked with the others, holding the baby's face above water.

"MELISSA?"

The spring on the screen door tightened, creaking open another notch.

Melissa struggled to keep her sister's face clear. The baby slipped through her wet hands, surfaced with a splash and began to choke. Melissa pushed her higher, her hands showing above the water.

"FAR-RAH," called the mother.

The cloud of bubbles increased as the jets swelled the pool. A mound of aeration foamed at the center.

The baby slid lower. Melissa's hands gripped tighter.

The water gushed and hissed. Steam snaked into the air. The screen door creaked, creaked again as if ticking the seconds.

At last Melissa came up gasping, hugging her sister against her, flinging water from her hair.

One by one the other heads came up.

"All right, who did that?"

"Shh, Melissa! Your mother—"

"I don't care! It's too late, anyway. Who's doing that? If you don't stop pushing me, Stacey, I'm never going to invite you—"

"But I didn't, Melissa. Somebody's touching me, too."

The hissing grew louder. The water churned

in the middle of the tub. There was a leaf,
bouncing on the surface. It skimmed the waves
like a silvered insect. And then—

There.

A shape.

A white mound came floating up from the
bottom, oily bubbles rolling off it. It was solid,
still fresh, moon-bleached, smoking. And
though it could not have been thrown into the
pool more than a couple of hours earlier, it was
now utterly and quite indisputably dead.

"Oh my God," said Melissa, "it—it's Shaun!
He's already here . . . !"

And then the baby was crying at the top of
her lungs and the others were screaming and
the back door slammed and more feet came
running and it was, it really was too late, after
all.

Call Home

When he walked in, the red light on the answering machine was blinking.

He dropped the mail on the coffee table and sat down. He ran a hand through his hair and leaned into the sofa, his ears still ringing from the rush-hour traffic.

He was in no hurry to replay his messages. It was easy to guess what they wanted: time, money, answers. He had none to spare. He reached out and stirred the pile of letters.

More of the same.

He got up, went to the bedroom and changed his clothes. Then he came back and sank deeper into the cushions. He propped his feet up and closed his eyes.

When the phone rang again, he let the machine take over.

"I'm not home right now," he heard his own recorded voice say, *"but if you care to leave a message, please begin speaking when you hear the tone. Thank you for calling. . . ."*

Beep.

A pause, and the incoming tape started rolling.

He waited to monitor the call.

Static. A rush of white noise. Like traffic.

No one there. Or someone who did not like talking to a machine.

A few more seconds and it would hang up automatically.

"Daddy? Is t-that you?"

He opened his eyes.

"Please c-can you come get me? I don't know how to get home . . . and I'm scared!"

What?

"It's getting cold . . . and dark . . ."

He sat forward.

"There's a man here . . . and he's bothering me! I think he's crazy! And it's going to rain and . . . and . . . Daddy, tell me what to do!"

He got to his feet.

"I don't like this place! There's a rooster . . . it's burning . . . and a gas station . . . and a sign. It says, um, it starts with a p. P-I-C-O . . ."

He crossed the living room.

"Daddy, please come quick . . . !"

He snatched up the receiver.

"Hello?" he said.

The child's voice began to sing brokenly.

"Ladybird, ladybird, fly away home . . . your house is on fire . . . and your children will burn. . . ."

Her voice trailed off as she started to cry.

"Hello? Hello?"

Click.

He stood there holding the phone, wondering what to do.

He was sure of only one thing.

He had no daughter.

So what if it was a wrong number? She was in trouble. A child, a little girl. What if something happened to her?

He couldn't let it go.

She had spelled out a word. P-I-C-O. The sign. A rooster, a gas station . . . yes, it sounded familiar.

The chicken restaurant. Next to the 76 station. On Pico Boulevard.

It wasn't far.

The traffic was still gridlocked. He crossed Wilshire in low gear, then Santa Monica, and turned west. A stream of cars growled past him, ragged music and demanding voices leaking from beneath shimmering hoods. He made a left on Westwood and kept to the right as he passed Olympic, slowing to a crawl as he came to the next corner.

She was huddled in the doorway of El Pollo Muerto, a school book bag at her feet. Her legs were dirty and her hair was in her eyes. A few yards away, at the gas station, was the phone booth. She did not look up as he braked by a loading zone.

He leaned over and rolled down the window. "Hey!"

The people at the bus stop glanced his way blankly, then stared past him down the street.

She lowered her head, resting her forehead on her arms.

He cleared his throat and shouted above the din. "Hey, little girl!"

She raised her head.

A woman eyed him suspiciously.

"Hi!" he called. "Hello, there! Do you need any help?"

The woman glared at him.

He ignored her and spoke to the girl.

"Are you the one who—?" Suddenly he felt foolish. "Did you call me?"

The little girl's face brightened.

"Daddy?"

The crowd moved closer. Then there was a rumbling and a pumping of brakes. He saw in his rearview mirror that an RTD bus had pulled up behind him.

"Come on," he said. "And your books—"

He opened the door for her as the bus sounded its horn.

"Daddy, it *is* you!"

The crowd surged past. The woman took notice of his license plate. The bus tapped his bumper.

"Get in."

He slipped into gear and got away from the curb. The pressure of traffic carried him across the intersection.

"Where do you want to go?" he asked. He passed another corner before it was possible to turn. "What's the address?"

"I don't know," said the little girl.

"You don't remember?"

She did not answer.

"Well, you'll have to tell me. Which way?"

"Want to go home," she said. She was now sitting straight in her seat, watching the lights with wide eyes.

"Are you all right?"

"I guess so."

At least it hasn't started to rain, he thought. "Did anyone hurt you?"

"I'm kind of hungry," she said.

He idled at a red light and got a good look at her. Seven, maybe eight years old and skinny as

Dennis Etchison

a rail. The bones in her wrists showed like white knuckles through the thin skin.

"When was the last time you had anything to eat?"

"I don't know."

She crossed her legs, angling a bruised ankle on a knobby knee, and he saw that her legs were streaked and smudged all the way up. My God, he thought, how long since she's had a bath? Had she been living on the streets?

"Well then," he said, "the first thing we'll do is get you some food." And then he would figure out what to do with her. "Okay?"

He took her to a deli. She gulped down a hot dog, leaving the bun on the plate, and watched him as he chewed his sandwich. He started to order her another, and realized something. He touched his hip pocket. Empty. He had forgotten his wallet when he changed his clothes.

"Take half of mine," he told her, trying to think.

"I don't like that kind."

She continued to watch him.

Finally he said, "Do you want another hot dog?"

"Yes, please!"

He ordered one more and saw to it that she drank her milk.

Afterward, while the waitress was in another

part of the restaurant, he said abruptly, "Let's go."

They drove away as the waitress came out onto the sidewalk.

"That was good," said the little girl.

"Glad you liked it. Now—"

"The way you did that. You didn't even leave a tip. You did it for me, didn't you?"

"Yes." What was I supposed to do? he thought. I'll come back tomorrow and take care of it. "Now where are we going?"

"Home," she said. "Oh, Daddy, you're so silly! Where did you think?"

"You've got to tell me," he said in the driveway.

"Tell you what?"

She got out and skipped to the front door, dragging her book bag. She waited for him on the porch.

He shook his head.

"Well," he said once they were inside, "are you going to tell me?"

"Um, where's the bathroom?"

"In there." He went to the phone. "But first—"

He heard water running.

He stood outside the bathroom door and listened. The shower was hissing, and presently she began to sing a song.

In the living room, the phone rang.

"I'm not home right now—"

"Jack, would you pick up, please? I know you're there. . . ."

"Hello, Chrissie. Sorry, I just got in."

"So late? Poor baby . . ."

"Listen, Chrissie, can I call you back? There's something I have to—"

"Are Ruth and Will there yet?"

"What?"

"Don't tell me you forgot! Well, I guess I can pick up something on the way over. You know, maybe we can get rid of them early. Would you like that?"

"Yeah, sure. But—"

"See you in a few minutes, love. And Jack? I've missed you . . . !"

Click.

"Daddy," called the little girl, "can you come here?"

He entered the darkened bedroom.

The bathroom door was open and steaming. She wrapped herself in a big towel and jumped up on the bed. She opened the towel.

"Dry me?"

"Listen," he said, "who told you to do this? I don't think it's such a good idea to—"

" 'S okay. I can do it myself." She made a few swipes with the towel and dropped it on the bed. Even in the faint light he could see how pink, how clean she was. And how small, and

how vulnerable. She lay down and wriggled under the sheet.

"Sleepy," she said.

He sat next to her, on the edge of the mattress.

"Kiss me good-night," she said. Her pale arms stretched out. He started to push her away, but she clung to him with all her might. He felt her tears as sobs wracked her body.

"There," he told her, patting her between sharp shoulder blades. "Shh, now . . ."

"Don't go," she said.

"I'm not going anywhere."

"Promise?"

"I promise."

He lay down next to her till her breathing became slow and regular. After a while he covered her with the blanket, and planted a kiss on her cool forehead before he left the room.

Ruth and Will parked behind Chrissie. He watched from the porch as they helped her carry the take-out food into the house.

He cleared his throat. "There's something I have to tell you."

"We already know," said Ruth.

"How?"

"They didn't hear it from me, I swear," said Chrissie.

Dennis Etchison

"A little bird told me," Ruth said. "And all I can say is, it's about time."

Will plopped down on the sofa. "Well, I think it's great. No point in paying rent on two places."

"*This* place sure isn't big enough," said Ruth. She stopped on the way to the kitchen and scanned the dining room. "Even if you got rid of these bookcases, it wouldn't work. You need more space."

"You know, Jack," said Will, "I have a friend in the real estate business. If you need any advice. Where's the Scotch?"

"Hold on . . ."

Chrissie winked at him as she passed. "They want to know if we've set the date. What do you think? Should we tell them everything?"

"Yes," he said.

"Wait a minute," said Will, rising and navigating for the bedroom door. "I want to hear this."

His stomach clenched. "Where are you going?"

Will grinned. "To take a leak. That all right with you?"

"Uh, would you mind using the other bathroom? This one's—stopped up."

Chrissie said, "It is? You didn't tell me that."

"I was going to. I was going to tell you all."

146

"Tell us what?" asked Ruth, coming out of the kitchen.

They looked at him expectantly. There was a long pause. His hands were shaking.

"I don't know where to start," he said. He tried a laugh but it came out wrong.

"Take your time," said Ruth. "We've got all evening."

Chrissie squeezed his arm. "Who needs a drink?" she said.

"Yes," he said. "Maybe we could have a drink first."

"What's this?" said Chrissie. She kicked the book bag on the floor, where the little girl had left it.

"Nothing," he said. "Here. Let me give you a hand."

He walked her to the kitchen.

"I can explain," he said.

"Explain what? You look tired, Jack. Was it an awful week?"

He took a deep breath. "Just this. I know it sounds crazy, but—"

On his way out of the small bathroom, Will stuck his head in the kitchen.

"Am I interrupting anything?"

"Of course not," said Chrissie.

"If this is a bad night for you two—"

There was a piercing scream from another part of the house.

He knew what it was before he got there.

The little girl was in the bedroom doorway, rubbing her eyes. She had on one of his shirts.

"Daddy?"

Ruth and Will looked at her. So did Chrissie. Then they looked at him.

"Oh, Daddy, there you are! I had a nightmare. There were people. Are they going now?"

"Daddy?" Chrissie stared at him as though she had never seen him before.

He focused on the little girl as his stomach clenched tighter.

"Tell them," he said.

"What?"

"Everything."

"I don't know what you mean, Daddy."

"All right," he said, "that's it. You're leaving—right now. I'll tell them the whole story myself. Come on. Let's go."

"No! I'll tell. How you picked me up at the bus stop and got me in the car in front of all those people? Or how you cheated and stole for me? Or the part where you gave me a bath and dried me and kissed me and we took a nap together?"

"I think we'd better be leaving," Ruth said.

"Yes," said Chrissie. "That might be a good idea. A very, very good idea."

"Wait." He followed her out. "Chris, I—"

"Don't," she said. "I have to think. And don't call me."

He watched numbly as the cars drove off. It started to rain softly, a misting drizzle in the trees above the mercury-vapor lamps. He watched until their red taillights turned the corner, like the reflection of a fire passing and moving on, leaving the street darker than ever.

"No," he said, hunching his shoulders. "No. No. No . . ."

He went back into the house.

"Where are you?" he shouted.

She was in the kitchen, helping herself to the food.

"Hi, Daddy," she said. "You got dinner for us. Just you and me. Thank you!"

"Who the hell do you think you are?"

He shook her violently.

"Daddy, you're hurting me!"

"I'm not your daddy and you know it, you little wretch."

"You're scaring me!"

"Don't bother to turn on the tears this time," he said. "It won't work."

She broke free and ran.

He braced himself against the table to stop shaking while he reached for the bottle of Scotch and poured a double shot.

Then he walked slowly, deliberately to the living room.

"Out," he said. "I don't care if it's raining. You've done enough. Get your things and—"

She had the phone in her hand.

"Daddy?" she said into the mouthpiece. "C-can you come and get me? I don't know how to get home . . . and I'm scared!"

He tried to take the phone away, but she dodged him and kept on talking.

"It's cold . . . and dark . . . and there's a man here . . . I think he's crazy! Daddy, tell me what to do! I don't like this place!"

She gave a description of his street.

"Daddy, please come quick!"

Then she began to sing sweetly, a high, plaintive keening like the wind outside, and the rain that blew with it, settling so coldly over the house.

"*Ladybird, ladybird, fly away home . . . your house is on fire . . . and your children will burn. . . .*"

Her voice trailed off as she started to cry.

She hung up. She stopped crying. Then she went about her business, collecting her clothing and her book bag as though he no longer existed.

He stood there, wondering what it was that was supposed to happen next.

No One You Know

This time the phone rang for ten minutes before she picked it up.

"Michael, stop. Or I'll call the police."

"We need to talk," he said.

She put the book down on the bed, took off her glasses and rubbed her eyes so hard that they made little squeaking sounds in their sockets.

"There's nothing to talk about."

"It wasn't what you think . . ."

"What was it, a mercy fuck?"

"I'm not going to lie to you. I made a mistake—*once*, that's all. It didn't mean anything . . ."

"I'm sure it didn't to her. What's thirty seconds, one way or the other?"

"You don't have to be nasty about it."

The young woman sighed, blowing air into the mouthpiece. She took the last of her Virginia Slims from a crumpled pack and searched the night table for a match.

"Oh, I get it," she said, "it's *my* fault now. You didn't do anything. You weren't even there, right?"

"One mistake and you're cutting me off. Just like that. I thought we had something . . ."

"Maybe we did, but it's over."

The cigarette hung from her lips at an odd angle. When she lit it nothing happened. There was a break in the middle and a thin stream of blue smoke wafted up and into her eyes before reaching her mouth. She dropped the match into a full ashtray but kept the cigarette clamped so tightly between her teeth that the filter deformed into a flattened oval.

"Listen . . ." he said.

"You just don't get it, do you? What is there about this that you can't understand? *Finis*. Do you hear what I'm saying?"

"Do you hear this?"

On the other end of the line, there was a click. She sighed again.

"It's one o'clock in the morning. Good night, Michael."

"Or *this*?" he said.

Then there was a second click, closer and sharper. It sounded like he had struck the mouthpiece with a pencil.

"What about it?" she said.

"That makes two out of six."

She opened her eyes and stared across the bedroom, trying to focus. The cigarette fell from her lips and onto the front of her night-gown. When she picked it up the teeth marks in the filter were so deep that it was bitten almost completely through, but she did not notice.

"Look, whatever your game is, I don't want to play, all right? I have to go to work in six hours . . ."

"This isn't a game," he said. "It's a matter of odds."

"What is?"

"I'm betting that you won't throw it all away."

"Don't be stupid."

"Then come over."

"What for?"

"We'll talk it out."

"I told you, no!"

"One more and it's fifty-fifty."

There was something different about his voice now. The tone was no longer smooth and conciliatory. It was not even desperate. It was mocking.

She sat up straight.

"What are you doing?"

"I'm a gambler, Jeannie. Are you?"

"What's that supposed to mean?"

"I always liked roulette. Here goes . . ."

"Wait."

"I could come over there."

"Do that and I call the police."

"Then listen up."

"Why?"

"I want you to hear it. So you'll never forget."

There was a third click in her ear, as loud as a piece of metal snapping. It must have been right next to his mouth.

"Michael, stop this! Whatever you're—"

"You lucked out," he said. "This time."

"I'm hanging up."

"You know I love you, don't you?"

"Good-*bye*!"

She broke the connection.

She dialed another number almost immediately.

"Mara, it's me."

"What time is it?"

"Sorry to bother you. I know it's late . . ."

"What's wrong?"

"Michael."

"Is he there?"

"No. But he won't give up."

"Just a minute." There was a faint clicking as

Mara turned on her lamp. "Now. What about Michael?"

"He wants to come over."

"The creep."

"I know. But he sounds like . . ."

"What?"

"I can't describe it. His voice isn't—normal."

"*He's* not normal. Get that through your head."

"He's doing something."

"Oh, dirty phone calls! Listen, girl, there's a law . . ."

"I just want him to leave me alone."

"I hear that."

"He's been calling all night."

"So take the phone off the hook."

"I can't."

"Why not?"

"I'm afraid of what he might to do."

"To you?"

"To himself."

"So let him! At least you'll get a good night's sleep."

"I can't, now."

"He isn't worth it, Jeannie."

"But what if he—does something?"

"That's your ego talking. This isn't about you. It could be anyone. He just likes the melodrama."

"I think he means it this time."

"Listen. He's a manipulator. He's trying to dominate you. It's the old passive-aggressive bit—control is the name of the game. Take my advice and don't play. Cut it off right now. Clean."

"I tried that. Only . . ."

"Only *what?* He's gambling on your weakness. Be strong. Once he finds out he can't make you jump anymore, he'll lose interest. Trust me."

"Maybe I should see him one more time," she said after a pause. "Just to be sure."

"Of what?"

"I don't know. That he's okay."

"You're crazy!"

"He only cheated once . . ."

"How do you know that?"

"We always told each other everything."

"Oh, really?"

"Well . . ."

"If he did it before, he'll do it again."

"He says it didn't mean anything."

"Sure. It was just his prick. Like it doesn't even belong to him. He found it in his pocket and thought he better try it out. What the hell."

"It's different for men."

"You got that right. They're not human."

"What's her name?"

"No one you know. Some bimbo with roots. Just his type."

"I think he has a gun."

"Did he threaten you?"

"No."

"Then he's just blowing smoke. Where would he get a gun?"

"His father's a cop. Was. He blew his brains out when Michael was nine."

"Don't worry about it. He doesn't have the guts. Besides, it's none of your business now. Do you hear what I'm saying?"

"I guess."

"You want to come over here?"

"I have to get up in the morning."

"Then take some NyQuil and zone out. Tomorrow you won't remember any of this."

"Are you sure?"

"I'm sure."

"Thanks, Mara."

"Anytime."

As soon as Mara put the phone down it rang again.

She tried to ignore it. She turned the TV on in her bedroom while the electronic chirping continued for another five minutes. When it finally stopped, she reached for the phone and punched in a series of numbers with such force that her long fingernail clicked against the keypad and left gouges in the plastic.

He answered right away.

"What is this bullshit about a gun?" she said.

"I knew it was you."

"You don't know jack shit. What are you trying to pull?"

"You talked to Jeannie."

"She's my best friend, remember?"

"I only called to see how she's doing."

"You lying sack of shit."

"I'm worried about her. I swear."

"Well, you can forget it. The girl is fine."

"Is that what she told you?"

"None of your business."

"She's unstable. When I told her I was through with her, she broke down."

"Give me a break!"

"We need to talk."

"You need to go fuck yourself."

"Just talk, that's all. I can be there in twenty minutes."

"You're certifiable, you know that?"

"What more do you want from me?"

"Don't even go there."

"Listen."

There was the sound of metal on metal.

"What are you doing?"

"Cocking the hammer."

"Don't you dare jerk me around! Your father was the one with the balls. Not you."

"This is number four."

"Michael—"

"One out of three, now. You like those odds?"

"Cut the crap or I'll call the cops! They'll put you in the psycho ward!"

"I only want to talk. You know I love you . . ."

"Go to hell."

She slammed down the phone.

He set the cordless telephone in front of him.

There was a notepad and pencil on the living room table, alongside a drinking glass, a fifth of Dewar's Scotch, a nickle-plated Smith & Wesson .38 Police Special and a box of Remington hollow-point cartridges. The top of the box was open. None of the rounds were missing.

He picked up the phone and entered a number.

When no one answered, he dialed a second number.

After a few minutes he put the handset down again, poured out an inch of the scotch, held it up in the light from the lamp and emptied the glass.

Then he took the Smith & Wesson in one hand. He swung the cylinder out, spun it with his other hand and sighted through the chambers to be sure they were all empty, then snapped it closed.

He laid it on the table and studied the notepad before taking up the phone again.

This time he got an answering machine.

Dennis Etchison

"Hi," he said. "I just wanted to see if you're all right. Oh, by the way, I didn't get the check. I thought you said you mailed it. If it doesn't get here by Wednesday, I'll have to come over. You don't want me to do that. Anyway, say hello to Dad for me. You know I love you, don't you, Mama?"

As he broke the connection, a white light swept over the front window.

He blinked and looked up.

Now red lights flashed on the other side of the curtains. They might have been taillights but it was hard to be sure.

He lifted the gun, opened it, inserted one of the cartridges and pointed the muzzle across the room.

A car door closed and footsteps started up the walk to the porch.

There was a knock on the door.

He drew the hammer back and waited, not moving a muscle.

The footsteps went away and passed along the side, down the driveway toward the back.

A moment later there was a click in another part of the house.

He turned around in his chair.

A shadow entered the living room from the kitchen.

He squinted into the darkness.

"Jesus," he said. "It's you."

"I used my key," she said.

"I thought you were going to call the cops."

"What do you think you're doing?"

"What do you care?"

She walked over to the table and stood looking down at him.

"I don't," she said. "I just wanted to be sure you're okay."

"I'm fine," he said, "now. I told you, it's over with her."

She saw the box of cartridges with one shell missing. "What the hell is this?"

"My dad's," he said.

"And this?" She reached for his arm under the table, where he had the pistol. "Give it to me."

"Want to play?"

"My God." Her eyes grew wide, then glassy as tears spilled down her cheeks. "It's true. Oh, my God."

He raised the gun.

She took a step back.

He eased the hammer back down, turned the gun around and held it out to her.

"Go ahead. If I can't have you, I don't care."

She snatched it from him and held it in front of her with both hands. Her knuckles were white.

"You're a player, aren't you?" he said. "It's still one out of two. Or two to one. I forget."

"I should do it," she said. She nodded at the

pad and pencil. "What's that, your suicide note? Perfect! I must have been out of my head. I only went to bed with you because you were so pathetic, always crying about her . . ."

"I told you, it's over. We don't have to sneak around anymore."

"I should fucking do it." Her face twisted up and she started to sob. "But I can't. I just can't . . ."

He closed the box of ammunition and placed it in the drawer, tore the top sheet off the notepad before she could see what was written there, crumpled it and dropped it into the wastebasket. Then he got out of the chair and faced her.

She stared at him, her lips trembling.

He took the gun from her.

"Stay," he said.

She kept staring, her eyes so bright that they seemed to give off sparks.

"God damn you," she said.

"We can talk about it in the morning."

She flung her keys down so hard that they gouged the floorboards and skittered away into the darkness.

Then she turned and crossed to the bedroom.

"Thanks for coming over," he said. "I can't stand to be alone. You know I love you, don't you, Mara?"

She slammed the door.

He smiled and threw his head back, laughing silently.

He started for the bedroom with a bounce in his step.

When he was halfway there he stopped and returned to the table. He reached down into the wastebasket and retrieved the sheet of paper from the pad. On it was written a list of women's names, at least a dozen of them, with telephone numbers after each one.

He smoothed the paper and slipped it into the drawer.

Then, just to be sure, he stuck the gun into the waistband at the back of his trousers before he followed her to the bedroom, closing the door behind him with a gentle click.

A Wind From The South

As Evie ran through the house, the morning light followed her. There was a white burst in each window, as if her passing had triggered a row of flashbulbs outside. Near the bedroom, she thought she saw a tall, dark outline squeeze from one pane to the next, pacing her, but the glass was so old that it flowed with distortion and she was unsure whether anyone was really there. It was not until she had peeled off her top and shorts and was about to step into the shower that the doorbell rang.

"Eddie, could you . . . ?"

But of course he couldn't. Her son had already gone, on his way to meet his friends and then to the mall.

"Dan?" she called, hoping that her husband would hear.

She stood with one hand on the hot water faucet and the other on the edge of the shower curtain, and waited. But Dan was still in the backyard. Too far away.

The bell rang again.

She reached for her robe. It was not on the back of the door. That's right, she thought, I put it in the laundry basket to be washed.

There was no time to get dressed. Should she ignore the bell? No, it might be United Parcel with a shipment intended for the store; then she or Dan would have to make a special trip just to pick it up.

She found his terrycloth robe in a heap at the end of the bed, where he had left it.

"Coming!" she shouted, tying the robe closed, and padded through to the living room.

She went first to the front window and peeked around the curtain. She could see only half of the porch, but it appeared to be empty, except for a long shadow cast by the overhang. Then something skittered across the lawn. She turned her head quickly, following a small pile of leaves that blew past on the sidewalk. Farther down the street, the mail truck rounded the corner, and a compact car idled under the stop sign. The car looked familiar. Was it Dan's?

That meant he had already left, without saying good-bye.

She let the curtain fall and opened the door. "Yes?"

A young woman stood there in profile, as though about to give up and move on. Beyond her, the lawn crackled with oak leaves. A wind had come up, as if from nowhere.

"I'm sorry to bother you," she said uncertainly, "but . . ."

Evie had never seen her before. At least there was no sample case in her hand; with any luck, she was not selling anything. That was a relief.

"It's all right," said Evie, relaxing slightly. "What can I—?"

"Well, you see . . ." She was hardly more than a girl, in her late teens or early twenties at most, though with the noonday sunlight behind her it was hard to be sure. Her hair was short and plain and she wore a loose, knee-length cotton dress several sizes too large, and no belt, as if to conceal her figure. "What street is this?" she asked finally.

"Stewart Way."

"Oh. I was afraid I took a wrong turn."

Did that mean she had, or hadn't?

"What address are you looking for?"

She had no reason to hide her body. From what Evie could see of her, long wiry arms, no stomach and short-toed pink feet, she was a perfect size four.

"I don't know. The school."

"Greenworth Elementary?" Was she walking? Barefoot? "You're almost there. Take a left at the corner, and then another left. You can't miss it."

"Thanks."

She made no move to leave, but lingered as though she had not yet said what was on her mind. Was she really going to the school? Maybe even a size two, thought Evie. I used to be that thin, once.

"Is there anything else?" Where was her watch? She had taken it off in the bathroom. "Because I'm kind of late. I was supposed to meet someone at twelve-thirty. For lunch." She gave the younger woman—girl?—a friendly but dismissive smile and started to shut the door.

"Is it far?"

"Just around the corner."

"I mean, where you're having lunch."

"What?" Evie wondered what business it was of hers. "Not really. Just over the hill."

"That's good." The girl looked at her wristwatch. "It's only eleven-fifteen."

"Is that all?" said Evie, surprised. "I thought it was twelve, at least."

The girl continued to stand there, the yellow-white light behind her, as the oak trees across the street shook down more leaves. Evie heard a scrabbling on the roof, twigs or tiny claws. The kitten? She felt a rush of radiant heat from the porch, moving the hair over her forehead, brushing the nap of her robe. Dan's robe. She retied it more securely.

"Do you think . . . ?"

"What?" asked Evie.

"Could I please have a drink of water? The wind, it's so hot . . ."

"It's a Santa Ana."

"A what?"

"It always comes this time of year."

"Why?"

She was not from around here. "I'm not sure. But it's a warm wind from the south—Mexico, I think. Below the border, anyway." As the trees rustled and waved, Evie opened the door wider. "You don't have to stand out there. Come in."

As she closed the door, the whispering chorus of leaves was silenced. Evie felt better; it had made her uneasy. Then she heard a ceiling beam creak, hammering into place over them. There was a faint scurrying from the fireplace as the wind rearranged the ashes in the grating. It had found a way to get into the house. She would have to tell Dan to close the flue.

"I'll get your water."

She started for the kitchen, then glanced back. The girl was standing awkwardly by the sofa. Was she looking for a place to sit? Evie paused to remove the morning newspaper from the cushions.

"My name's Eve, by the way. Eve Markham."

"I know."

She was dark, probably Hispanic, Evie noticed. Or was it only a deep tan? "How?"

"From the mailbox."

The odd moment passed as easily as a skipped heartbeat.

She expected the girl to offer her own name in return.

She waited.

"Oh," Evie said after a few seconds. "Well, hi."

"Hi."

She went to the kitchen, took down one of the tall glasses, filled it quickly and returned. "I didn't ask if you wanted ice."

"What? Oh, no. This is fine." The girl took a sip, that was all, and set the glass on the table in front of her.

She was seated comfortably on the sofa and the hastily-piled newspapers were nowhere to be seen. Had she moved them? Where? Evie wondered if she might be a housekeeper, looking for a job. But that made no sense. Why this house? Evie put it out of her mind.

"Do you live in the neighborhood?" Evie asked, sitting down in the easy chair.

"I'll be moving in soon. As soon as I find the right place."

Evie heard a car pass through the intersection at the corner, going away. She lowered her eyes while she tried to think of something else to say, and saw her knees poking out under the robe, as though it were not Dan's but her own short one instead. She covered her legs, and noted the backs of her hands. They made her look older, middle-aged. She was aware of the blood pulsing in her wrists, which were glistening. She touched her face, her neck. Her skin felt hot. It must have been the wind. Now she needed that shower more than ever. Why was there no clock in the living room?

"You have a child at the elementary school?" she asked.

"Not yet. I wanted to see the other children first. Is that when they have their lunch, at noon?"

It had been so long—a year? no, more—since her own son had gone there that Evie could hardly remember. The school was close enough that Eddie had come home for lunch most days, even when she and Dan were at work.

"I think so. But there aren't any classes today, only the play group."

The girl took another small sip of her water. Was there something wrong with it? Sorry I don't have bottled, Evie thought.

"You'll have to excuse me," she said, "but I really should—"

There was a wrenching sound from the backyard, and something fell with a terrible crash.

She hurried through the long house to the back porch.

The yard looked different somehow; at first she could not be sure why. For one thing, there was more sky showing than there should have been. Then she realized that one of the trees Dan had planted between the house and the garage had fallen over. No, not fallen but broken, the top half lying in a pile of dry, misshapen branches and withered, unborn fruit, near the two dwarf palms. The trunk was split sharply and the bark stripped back to expose the soft white center, like a ragged piece of chicken meat that has been peeled away from the bone.

The girl was right behind her.

"The tree," said Evie. "I can't believe it. At least it didn't hit the house."

"Was it the wind?"

"Yes, I suppose so." What else?

"I'm sorry."

"That's all right. It's not your fault! He should have watered it more."

"Who?"

"Dan. My husband."

"I didn't see his name on the mailbox."

It was there. Dan & Eve Markham. She remembered the day he placed the adhesive letters on the box at the curb. He had done that, hadn't he? Unless they had peeled off.

She considered the broken tree, and felt a pang of sadness. They had neglected the backyard for so long. Once there had been a garden, lush and vibrant. How many years ago? With all the dead plants, and now this, it looked more like a cemetery overrun with weeds. But there was nothing to do about it now.

"Dan won't be very happy, when he gets home."

"What does your husband do?" asked the girl, as they walked back to the living room.

"He has a bookstore—we do. New and used. Minor Arcana, on Main and Second."

"Is that where he is now?"

"I hope not. This is his day off." Mine, too, she thought. At least it was supposed to be.

Still, it was good that she was not alone. If she had not answered the doorbell, she would have been in the shower when it happened. She imagined herself running through the house at the sound of the crash, dripping water.

"I'm glad you were here," Evie said.

"So am I."

"Do you want more water?"

"He must be very smart, your husband."

Evie laughed, releasing the tension. "He's the most intelligent man I ever met. That's why I married him. Or one of the reasons."

"Did he get his degree?"

"Well, not quite. He spent years at college, but he never graduated. He only took the classes he liked." It seemed a peculiar question. "What about your husband?"

"He has his own business. And he's very smart, too. We're going to have a nice house, with lots of windows, just like this one. As soon as we get settled."

Evie leaned back in the chair and took a better look at the younger woman. Actually she might not have been so young, after all; it was hard to tell. Her hair was unstylish, as if she had cut it herself and was now waiting to see how it would grow out. The windows were behind the sofa so that her features were backlighted, neutral, but Evie was sure that she wore no makeup. Her legs were strong and well-shaped, with small ankles. And there was the wristwatch, a man's Swiss Army model, above her left arm. But no ring.

She met dozens of people every day, many absolute strangers who came into the store in search of a book. Some of them did not know the name of the author or the title, or even what exactly they were looking for. Evie knew how to talk to them, to put them at their ease and make them feel comfortable, to draw them out and learn what they were really after. Sometimes they did not want anything but conversation. In that case she still tried to satisfy them before sending them on their way, so that they would come back. Now, however, she was not in the shop, and this was not a customer. What the young woman wanted was unclear. Evie felt at a disadvantage. This one knew the power of silence. It was a way of maintaining the upper hand. But for what purpose?

"So you have children of your own?" Of course she does, Evie thought. She hadn't said so, not exactly, but why else would she be interested in the school?

"Do you?"

"One son," said Evie. "His name's Edward. He just turned thirteen."

She decided to leave it at that. Her natural impulse would have been to tell the woman all about Eddie, as much as she could stand to hear, his brilliance and precocity. But now for some reason she felt instinctively protective. She was relieved that he was not here.

"Is he at school?"

"Not today. It's Saturday. Remember?"

"Then where?"

Evie was conscious of a chill in the air. She fingered the edge of the robe, pulling it closed at her throat.

"With a friend." Yes, the Oshidari boy, over on Bradfield. That was right, wasn't it?

"Is your husband coming back?"

"Of course he is. Why wouldn't he?"

"I'd like to . . . meet him."

Evie stood. "Excuse me. I have to get ready now."

"Are you sure?"

What did that mean? "I'm afraid so. It's late."

"Is it?"

Danny, she thought, where are you? "What does that watch of yours say?"

The woman looked at her wrist. She tapped the crystal. "It stopped."

"When?"

"I don't know."

Evie went to the bedroom doorway and peered in at the clock on the nightstand.

"It's twelve-thirty!" she said.

"You should have a watch."

"I do," Evie snapped. "I took it off for my shower, and then you rang the bell."

"You need a clock in the living room. I'm going to have one, in my new house."

Evie pulled the front door wide. "I'm sure you will," she said. "Good-bye."

In the bedroom, she glanced around for some sign of her husband's clothes, even his socks by the bed, but they were not there. They were with the laundry, waiting to be washed. Weren't they? She had the urge to go to the back porch, where the washer and dryer were, just to be sure. There was no time. But if she did, she could look in at her son's room on the way. Why? To see that his clothes, his possessions were still there? She scanned the empty bedroom, frantic. Where were her son's childhood drawings? She had taped them to the wall years ago, hadn't she? *Hadn't she?*

She felt fear then, rising up through her body, going for her throat. Her hands clenched into fists, her fingers so small, her knuckles white as bones ready to pop through the skin. Where was her ring? Had she taken it off in the bathroom?

She struggled to form a name on her lips. Dan, she thought. That was it. And the name of her son. Edward.

Where were they?

A warm wind filled the room, flushing her cheeks.

The front door, she realized. She had left it open.

She went back to the living room.

There was the woman, in the doorway. She was standing in profile again, the hot wind blowing past her into the house, catching her dress so that it billowed out from her body. Now, the dress inflated with air, she appeared to be much heavier, by twenty or thirty pounds at least. The heat blurred, creating a mirage between Evie and the door, so that the woman's legs seemed suddenly thick, grown strong enough to carry the added weight, her ankles swollen and bloated.

"What do you want from me?" Evie said, reeling.

The hot wind subsided, moving on, and something left the house. The woman's dress deflated, hanging once more in loose folds. But, as Evie watched, she saw with perfect clarity that the woman was no longer slender. The front of the dress remained distended like a balloon, straining to cover a round, unmistakably swollen belly, where before it had been absolutely flat and empty.

"Nothing," said the other woman, and twisted the gold ring on her left hand. Then she turned to leave at last, smiling as if she had a secret, something too new and too personal, too private to share with anyone, least of all a stranger, just yet.

The Scar

This time they were walking a divided highway, the toes of their shoes powdered white with gravel dust. The little girl ran ahead, skipping eagerly along the shoulder, while her mother lagged back to keep pace with the man.

"Mind the trucks," called the woman, barely raising her voice. Soon the girl would be able to take care of herself; that was her hope. She turned to him, showing the good side of her face. "Do you see one yet?"

He lifted his chin and squinted.

She followed his gaze to the other side of the highway. There, squatting in the haze beyond the overpass, was a Weenie Wigwam Fast Food Restaurant.

"Thank God," she said. She thought of the Chinese Smorgasbord, the Beef Bowl, the Thai Take-Out and the many others they had seen already. She added, "This one will be all right, won't it?"

It was the edge of the town, RV dealerships and fleet sales on one side of the road, family diners and budget motels on the other. Overloaded station wagons and moving vans laden with freight hammered the asphalt, bringing thunder to the gray twilight. Without breaking stride the man leaned down to scoop up a handful of gravel, then skimmed stones between the little girl's thin legs and into the ditch; he held onto one last piece, a sharp quartz chip, and deposited it in his jacket pocket.

"Maybe," he said.

"Aren't you sure?"

He did not answer.

"Well," she said, "let's try it. Laura will be hungry, I know."

She hurried to catch the little girl at the crossing. When she turned back, the man was handling an empty beer bottle from the roadside. She looked away. As he moved up to join them, zippering the front of his service jacket, the woman forced a smile, as if she had not seen.

*   *   *

In the parking lot, the man took their hands. A heavy tanker geared down and pounded the curve, bucking and hissing away behind them. As it passed, the driver sounded his horn at the traffic. The sudden blast, so near that it rattled her spine, seemed to release her from a bad dream. She laced her fingers more securely with his and swung her arm out and back and out again, hardly feeling the weight of his hand between them.

"This is a nice place," she said, already reading a banner for the all-day breakfast special. "I'm glad we waited. Aren't you glad, Laura?"

"Can I ride the horse?" asked the little girl.

The woman looked at the sculpted gray-and-white Indian pinto, its blanket saddle worn down to the fiberglass. There were no other children waiting at the machine. She let go of his hand and dug in her purse for a coin.

"I don't see why not," she said.

The little girl broke away.

He came to a stop, his empty hands opening and closing.

"Just one ride," the woman said quickly. "And then you come right inside, hear?"

On the other side of the glass, couples moved between tables. A few had children, some Laura's age. Families, she thought. She wished that the three of them could go inside together.

Laura's pony began to wobble and pitch. But

the man was not watching. He stood there with his chin up, his nostrils flared, like an animal waiting for a sign. His hands continued to flex.

"I'll see about a table," she said when he did not move to open the door.

A moment later she glanced outside and saw him examining a piece of brick that had come loose from the front of the restaurant. He turned it over and over.

The menus came. They sat reading them in a corner booth, under crossed tomahawks. The food items were named in keeping with the native American motif, suggesting that the burgers and the several varieties of hot dogs had been invented by hunters and gatherers. Bleary travelers hunched over creased roadmaps, gulping coffee and estimating mileage, their eyes stark in the chill fluorescent lighting.

"What would you like, Laura?" asked the woman.

"Peanut butter and jelly sandwich."

"Do they have that?"

"And a vanilla milkshake."

The woman sighed.

"And Wampum Pancakes. Papoose-size."

She opened her purse and counted the money. She blinked and looked at the man.

He got up and went over to the silverware station.

"What's he doing?" said the little girl.

"Never mind," said the woman. "His knife and fork must be dirty."

He came back and sat down.

"And Buffalo Fries," said the little girl.

The woman studied him. "Is it still okay?" she asked.

"What?" he said.

She waited, but now he was busy observing the customers. She gave up and returned to the menu. It was difficult for her to choose, not knowing what he would order. "I'll just have a small dinner salad," she said at last.

The others in the restaurant kept to themselves. A man with a sample case ate a piece of pecan pie and scanned the local newspaper. A young couple fed their baby apple juice from a bottle. A take-away order was picked up at the counter, then carried out to a Winnebago. Soft, vaguely familiar music lilted from wall speakers designed to look like tom-toms, muffling the clink of cups and the murmur of private conversations.

"Want to go to the bathroom," said the little girl.

"In a minute, baby," the woman told her. A waitress in an imitation buckskin mini-dress was coming this way.

The little girl squirmed. "Mom*my!*"

The waitress was almost here, carrying a

pitcher and glasses of water on a tray.

The woman looked at the man.

Finally he leaned back and opened his hands on the table.

"Could you order for us?" she asked carefully.

He nodded.

In the rest room, she reapplied make-up to one side of her face, then added another layer to be sure. At a certain angle the deformity did not show at all, she told herself. Besides, he had not looked at her, really looked at her in a long time; perhaps he had forgotten. She practiced a smile in the mirror until it was almost natural. She waited for her daughter to finish, then led her back to the dining room.

"Where is he?" said the little girl.

The woman tensed, the smile freezing on her lips. He was not at the table. The food on the placemats was untouched.

"Go sit down," she told the little girl. "Now."

Then she saw him, his jacket with the embroidered patches and the narrow map like a dragon on the back. He was on the far side of the room, under a framed bow and arrow display.

She touched his arm. He turned too swiftly, bending his legs, his feet apart. Then he saw who it was.

"Hi," she said. Her throat was so dry that her

voice cracked. "Come on, before your food gets cold."

As she walked him to the table, she was aware of eyes on them.

"I had a bow and arrow," he said. "I could pick a sentry out of a tree at a hundred yards. Just like that. No sound."

She did not know what to say. She never did. She gave him plenty of room before sitting down between him and the little girl. That put her on his other side, so that he would be able to see the bad part of her face. She tried not to think about it.

He had only coffee and a small sandwich. It took him a while to start on it. Always travel light, he had told her once. She picked at her salad. The people at the other tables stopped looking and resumed their meals.

"Where's my food?" asked the little girl.

"In front of you," said the woman. "Now eat and keep quiet."

"Where's my pancakes?"

"You don't need pancakes."

"I do, too!"

"Hush. You've got enough." Without turning her face the woman said to the man, "How's your sandwich?"

Out of the corner of her eye she noticed that he was hesitating between bites, listening to the sounds of the room. She paused, trying to hear what he heard. There was the music, the undercurrent of voices, the occasional ratcheting of the cash register. The swelling traffic outside. The chink of dishes in the kitchen, as faint as rain on a tin roof. Nothing else.

"Mommy, I didn't get my Buffalo Fries."

"I know, Laura. Next time."

"When?"

She realized she did not know the answer. She felt a tightening in her face and a dull ache in her throat so that she could not eat. Don't let me cry, she thought. I don't want her to see. This is the best we can do—can't she understand?

Now his head turned toward the kitchen.

From behind the door came distant clatter as plates were stacked, the squeak of wet glasses, the metallic clicking of flatware, the high good humor of unseen cooks and dishwashers. The steel door vibrated on its hinges.

He stopped chewing.

She saw him check the room one more time: the sharply-angled tables, the crisp bills left for tips, the half-eaten dinners hardening into waste, the full bellies and taut belts and bright new clothing, too bright under the harsh fixtures as night fell, shuttering the windows with leaden darkness. Somewhere outside headlights gathered as vehicles jammed the turnoff, stabbing the glass like approaching search-lights.

He put down his sandwich.

The steel door trembled, then swung wide.

A shiny cart rolled into the dining room, pushed by a busboy in a clean white uniform. He said something over his shoulder to the kitchen crew, rapid-fire words in a language she did not understand. The cooks and dishwashers roared back at his joke. She saw the tone of their skin, the stocky, muscular bodies behind the aprons. The door flapped shut. The cart was coming this way.

He spat out a mouthful of food as though afraid that he had been poisoned.

"It's okay," she said. "See? They're Mexicans, that's all. . . ."

He ignored her and reached inside his jacket. She saw the emblems from his Asian tour of duty. But there were also patches from Tegu-cigalpa and Managua and the fighting that had gone on there. She had never noticed these before. Her eyes went wide.

The busboy came to their booth.

Under the table, the man took something from his pants pocket and set it beside him on the seat. Then he took something else from the other side. Then his fists closed against his knees.

"Can I have a bite?" said the little girl. She

started to reach for the uneaten part of his sandwich.

"Laura!" said the woman.

"Well, he doesn't want it, does he?"

The man looked at her. His face was utterly without expression. The woman held her breath.

"Excuse," said the busboy.

The man turned his head back. It seemed to take a very long time. She watched, unable to stop any of this from happening.

When the man did not say anything, the busboy tried to take his plate away.

A fork came up from below, glinted, then arced down in a blur, pinning the brown hand to the table.

The boy cried out and swung wildly with his other hand.

The man reached under his jacket again and brought a beer bottle down on the boy's head. The boy folded, his scalp splitting under the lank black hair and pumping blood. Then the cart and chairs went flying as the man stood and grabbed for the tomahawks on the wall. But they were only plastic. He tossed them aside and went over the table.

A waitress stepped into his path, holding her palms out. Then she was down and he was in the middle of the room. The salesman stood up, long enough to take half a brick in the face.

Then the manager and the man with the baby got in the way. A sharp stone came out, and a lockback knife, and then a water pitcher shattered, the fragments carrying gouts of flesh to the floor.

The woman covered her little girl as more bodies fell and the room became red.

He was going for the bow and arrow, she realized.

Sirens screamed, cutting through the clot of traffic. There was not much time. She crossed the parking lot, carrying the little girl toward the Winnebago. A retired couple peered through the windshield, trying to see. The child kicked until the woman had to put her down.

"Go. Get in right now and go with them before—"

"Are you going, too?"

"Baby, I can't. I can't take care of you anymore. It isn't safe. Don't you understand?"

"Want to stay with you!"

"Can we be of assistance?" said the elderly man, rolling down his window.

She knelt and gripped the little girl's arms. "I don't know where to go," she said. "I can't figure it out by myself." She lifted her hair away from the side of her face. "Look at me! I was born this way. No one else would want to help us. But it's not too late for you."

189

Dennis Etchison

The little girl's eyes overflowed.

The woman pressed the child to her. "Please," she said, "it's not that I want to leave you . . ."

"We heard noises," said the elderly woman. "What happened?"

Tall legs stepped in front of the camper, blocking the way.

"Nothing," said the man. His jacket was torn and spattered. He pulled the woman and the little girl to their feet. "Come on."

He took them around to the back of the lot, then through a break in the fence and into a dark field, as red lights converged on the restaurant. They did not look back. They came to the other side of the field and then they were crossing the frontage road to a maze of residential streets. They turned in a different direction at every corner, a random route that no one would be able to follow. After a mile or so they were out again and back to the divided highway, walking rapidly along in the ditch.

"This isn't the way," said the little girl.

The woman took the little girl's hand and drew her close. They would have to leave their things at the motel and move on again, she knew. Maybe they would catch a ride with one of the truckers on the interstate, though it was hard to get anyone to stop for three. She did not know where they would sleep this time; there wasn't enough left in her purse for another room.

"Hush, now." She kissed the top of her daughter's head and put an arm around her. "Want me to carry you?"

"I'm not a baby," said the little girl.

"No," said the woman, "you're not. . . ."

They walked on. The night lengthened. After a while the stars came out, cold and impossibly distant.

The Detailer

Paulino was whistling by the time he got to work.

He could not remember the name of the song. It had started running through his head as soon as the alarm went off, and then he heard it in the shower and all through breakfast. When Rosalie asked him why he was so happy he told her he didn't know, but he kept on hearing the song until finally he began to whistle. He had to let it out, like steam.

On the way the streets were jammed and the air was so brown that the sun was only a pale, dirty glint. He kept his window rolled up and tried to think of the words but he could not get the first line.

Ruben was in the driveway of the Palm Vista Car Wash, setting out the *Yes, We're Ready for Your Dirt* sign. He had a blue towel in the pocket of his clean white jumpsuit and an expression on his face that would not give him away. Paulino rolled the window down.

"Little Paulie," said Ruben.

"O Rosalinda—she won, right?"

"Yeah, by a nose."

Paulino grinned and turned up the driveway. He parked his Ford Escort and hurried back to the building, whistling louder than ever. Ruben was inside at the snack machines.

"How much?"

"Twelve-to-one," said Ruben.

"All right!"

"I had forty . . ."

"And forty for me."

"But, see, I got there late. The race already started. They closed the window."

"No la!"

Ruben fumbled coins into the soda machine, missed the Pepsi button and hit Mr. Pibb instead. "I'll pay you back."

"You don't even have my forty?"

"My kids, they ate a lot of crap. Two-fifty for a hot dog. Plus nachos and Cokes. You know."

Paulino turned away, went to another machine and waited while a paper cup dropped and filled with coffee. He stirred in some creamer, breathing the steam while it cooled. Then he heard the water come on and the shammies start to move in the car wash tunnel. When he felt the rhythm through the thick soles of his shoes he thought of the song again. He could still make it out over the wet, grinding rhythm.

"Okay, *compá*," he said. "Friday for sure . . ."

But Ruben was already outside, guiding the first car onto the automated track. It was an Isuzu Rodeo so new it glistened before it got to the jets.

Paulino finished the coffee, punched his time card and put on his jumpsuit.

He saw the Rodeo disappear as the wall of shammies closed over the back end. Then foam spurted as the soap hit the rear tires. The sidewalls were black and gleaming and there was still a dealer card in the license plate holder. This one was not ready to be washed. The paint had not even set. It only needed a dusting to take off the pollution from the air.

But at Palm Vista the customer was king.

He looked around to see who owned it. Several people already had receipts from the glass office. He recognized a half dozen regulars, businessmen and college students and mothers on their way back from the elementary school, ready to start the week off right.

There was Mrs. McLintock, who took such good care of her old Pontiac that it shone even in the overcast. Jason, the kid with the Cabrio and the UCLA parking permit. And Cheryl, who had a smile to match her bright yellow Beetle. She spent a lot of time at the beach, he knew, because there was always sand in the floor mats. And Mr. Travis, who had just traded up his Camry for an Audi A4. Paulino wondered how he liked it.

He would have to ask.

It cost nothing to make conversation with the customers, and besides, Mr. Travis was his friend. They all were. They called him by name, telling him to be careful about the grocery bags in the back seat and could he make sure to get the rearview mirror because it fogged up last night on the way home and they almost had an accident. When he did these special things for them they tipped him extra, and when they forgot he would talk about something else till they remembered, and if they didn't have any small bills he would tell them to catch him next time and they usually did. It was only fair. He listened to their problems and did his best to make them happy and that was worth something. A clean car gave them another chance at life. They understood that and kept coming back. This morning the sedans and station wagons and sport utility vehicles were backed up into the alley. They could hardly wait.

A new customer was hanging around the tables, a salesman in a short-sleeved dress shirt and polyester tie with blue and white stripes. He kept checking his watch. That's the one with the Rodeo, Paulino thought. It has to be. He looks like he just started a new job and he's worried sick about making a good impression. Well, you can relax, *vato*. I'm ready to straighten your tie and wash behind your ears and polish your chrome before you go out into the world. Leave it to Paulie.

He picked up his detail kit and walked down to the other end of the tunnel to meet the Rodeo when it came out.

Ruben was inside with Manny and the others, sponging the hubcaps as the vehicle went by, wiping the grille and the door handles till they shone like liquid silver. The next car was moving up behind it, Cheryl's Beetle with the happy face front-end. Paulino watched the Rodeo pass under the hot-wax nozzles, then got into the front seat and steered it over the blacktop to the vacuum hoses.

He set the brake, suctioned the new floor mats and polished the mirror and instrument panel while he waited for the water to drain off the hood. He checked the ashtray, saw a few coins and a paperclip there and slid it back in without disturbing them, then sprayed silicone protectant over the dash and rubbed it to a deep luster. That was an extra. The salesman had only paid for a basic wash and hot wax, but Paulino knew he would appreciate it. Cheryl's car always got the same treatment. She never paid for detailing, either. But if he and Rosalie had a daughter he hoped she would grow up with a smile just like that.

He climbed out of the Rodeo and set to work on the rubber trim before the water spots burned in, and heard music again.

It was not the same song. This time there was a heavy, throbbing bass line, very close by. He glanced up, almost expecting to see a thunderhead on the horizon behind the marquee. The moveable letters spelled out this week's slogan, *No Job's Too Dirty for Us*. Beyond that he saw only the power lines and the signal lights at the corner and the hot disk of the sun about to break through the smog. The pressure in his ears grew stronger.

He looked out at the smear of cars on the street, locked bumper-to-bumper as the traffic inched past. A Buick Regal and a Crown Vic LTD pulled even at the red light, sub-woofers booming, shaking the hoods with each beat like two hearts at war. The radios drowned out the song in his mind. He turned his back on the street and hunkered down behind the Rodeo, sprayed Armor All on the molded bumper, and wondered why Rosalie never woke up with music in her head.

There was no time for that, she had said in the kitchen, especially not on a Monday. What was wrong with him? Did he think she liked spending all day cleaning other people's houses? The things they left for her were disgusting, things they wouldn't touch themselves, things she had never thought she'd have to touch when she came here, after he had promised her so much. Well, he said, maybe you should go home and visit your family for a week, two weeks, he didn't care, and that was what tore it. When she started crying he did not say anything else. She would not even let him kiss her when he dropped her off.

He finished wiping down the Rodeo.

Ruben was working on the yellow Beetle, Manny had the Audi and Craig was about to start on Mrs. McLintock's cherry Pontiac. She was already opening her purse for a tip that could have been Paulino's. He hoped she and Mr. Travis and Cheryl did not think he was avoiding them. If he had not spent so much time on the Rodeo he would be ready. The line moved forward and two more cars from the alley were about to enter the tunnel.

The salesman checked his watch nervously and shifted his weight in tight brown shoes. Paulino ran his towel over the windows, brushed out the front seat, waved him over and handed him the keys.

The salesman got in without a word.

"Nice car," said Paulino.

The salesman inserted his key.

"You want to be careful with that clear-coat, though. It scratches real easy." Paulino closed the door in slow motion, holding onto it as long as he could. "You put on some sealer and glaze, you won't have to worry."

"It's a lease," said the salesman.

"Yeah, well, just the same, I'd get a full detail. Say every sixty to ninety days. You need it around here."

"Thanks for the advice."

"Hey, no problem. Just ask for Paulie."

The salesman got the message. He reached into his pocket and pulled out a dollar bill before he turned the key.

"I'll think about it."

"I only use Mother's Gold." Paulino winked and showed the man his teeth. "One-hundred-percent pure carnauba. Guaranteed."

The salesman started the engine and drove away.

Paulino saw Craig folding paper money into his pocket and thought, I should get some cards printed up. It wouldn't cost much. Plain white business cards, with my name, and underneath that *The Detailer*. And maybe my phone number, too, so I can make house calls on my day off. Why not?

He picked up his kit.

On the way to the glass office he asked Mrs. McLintock how she was doing today. She beamed as if he were her favorite son. He said hello to Mr. Travis, who told him the A4 was the best car he had ever owned. When he came up behind Cheryl she was digging out some loose change for Manny.

"How's the Vee-Dub?"

"Great! Hi, Paulie. I missed you!"

"You oughta let me get those wheels."

"Well . . ."

Paulino frowned. "See, they're alloy. All that nitrous from the diesels, it wrecks the aluminum. If you don't do nothing about it, you got a problem. I can put on some Wheel Brite . . ."

"I'm late for class. Will you be here, um, Thursday?"

"Sure. Any time."

"Cool. See you then!"

She grinned and gave a little wave with her fingers.

At the office he held his kit up so Linda the cashier could see the cans of wax and polish through the glass and shrugged at her. She pointed to the job board and shook her head. No one had signed up for detailing so far, just washes and spray wax.

It was going to be a slow morning.

He took a copy of the *Times* from the counter

and went back to see who else was waiting. Mr. Nolan was at the tables, sipping black coffee and eating a donut from the Winchell's on the corner. His Geo Metro had not been hand-waxed all year. Paulino was about to bring him the newspaper, when he spotted a metallic grey Lexus LX420 in the driveway. It had just moved forward from the alley and was next in line.

That would be Mrs. Ellsworth.

He smiled and gave her the high sign.

When there was no response he went to the driveway and stood before the tinted windshield, motioning for her to get out so he could take it the rest of the way. 4SUZIE, said the license plate on the front bumper. He knew whose it was without looking. The vehicle came in once a week like clockwork.

The door opened and a man with dark glasses climbed down.

"Oh," said Paulino. "Morning, Mr. Ellsworth. The usual?"

"Not this time."

"You don't want the wash and hot wax?"

"Give me the works."

Paulino was confused. "You mean a full detail?"

The man nodded and pushed his glasses farther up his nose so that no part of his eyes showed. "Get this baby clean, inside and out."

Paulino had given the Lexus a complete detail

only last Monday, when Mrs. Ellsworth brought it in right on schedule. A perfect layer of wax still showed through the mud spatters on the fenders. There was some dirt clinging to the sidewalls that would come off as soon as the spray hit them. But the customer was king.

"It'll take about an hour . . ."

"I'll wait."

Mr. Ellsworth had never waited around for the detailing. When he first got the Lexus he used to drop it off on Mondays and his wife would drive him the rest of the way to his office in the LS400, but after a while he started taking the sedan so that she could use the sport utility. She brought the LX420 in every week for a wash and one Monday a month for a detail. It was her responsibility now, not his.

"Okay," said Paulino, to be sure he understood. "Wheels, trim, upholstery, hand-wax . . ."

"Forget the wax."

"Steam-clean the engine?"

Mr. Ellsworth shook his head impatiently. "I don't give a damn. Just make everything look fresh as a daisy. Got it?"

"Yes, sir," said Paulino.

"You'll take care of it for me." The man slipped a hundred-dollar bill out of his wallet. "Won't you."

"Sure, Mr. Ellsworth." Without the hand-wax and steam-clean, that was more than enough. A lot more. Paulino took the bill and started for the office. "I'll get your change."

"The car, first."

"No problem." It was too early for Paulino to break a large bill. He would take it in to Linda when he finished. "Did you have a nice vacation?"

"What?"

"Triangle Lake."

"How do you know about that?"

"Mrs. Ellsworth . . ." Paulino faltered. "She said you were going on a trip. For the weekend."

"We didn't go anywhere."

"Oh, too bad. I hear it's really great up there. All those trees and everything. Some other time, huh?"

The man pushed his glasses up his nose again, so hard that his hand trembled.

"There was no trip."

"Yes, sir, Mr. Ellsworth."

Paulino put his kit in the back seat and got behind the wheel.

As he steered the car forward the front wheels made contact with the track and the strips of wet cloth begin to sway from side to side. Then the rollers tripped the sensor and the first nozzles sprayed foam at the tires.

He saw the next line of flaps closing over the Metro ahead of him as the ceiling jets went on. The water was a falling black mist in the tunnel.

He felt himself drawn into the darkness, heard the wet ratcheting of the machinery all around and checked to see that the windows were tightly closed, then remembered to get out now before it was too late. Otherwise he would have to ride it out to the end, trapped. This was not Paulino's job. He was the one who finished up after the heavy dirt had been washed away. Let the others take care of that. His work was to make things pretty again, at least the parts that showed. He opened the door and jumped down before the shammies touched the windshield.

He stepped around Manny, heading for the square of daylight at the end of the tunnel.

"Where's Suzie Q?"

"Mrs. Ellsworth?"

"The Body!" said Manny. He had to shout over the hissing water. "The one with the headlights!"

"She didn't come in."

As the sport utility vehicle crept by, Ruben snapped his rag at a crust of dirt on the tailpipe. "Aw, I been waiting all week!"

"Maybe she's sick," said Paulie.

"Or she got a new boyfriend!"

"Too much dick last night!" said Craig.

They laughed.

Paulino made his way through the tunnel and waited for the sport utility to roll off the track.

Dennis Etchison

Then he started it up and drove a few feet to the hoses.

He did not like to hear them talk that way. Mrs. Ellsworth had posed for some magazines a few years ago but it stopped when she got married. She was a nice person. She always stood around even in her high heels and talked to him while she waited. They had some good conversations. On the Mondays when he did the detailing he had a chance to learn all about her.

He removed the beads of water with a clean blue towel, then opened the doors and got started with the vacuum.

She probably told him too much. About her marriage, for example. Paulino knew it was not going great. That was easy to understand. Sometimes people want different things. They don't tell each other before they get married and by the time it comes out it's too late. Then they just have to do the best they can and hope everything gets better.

Paulino swiped the vacuum between the seats, heard a flapping sound and stopped. A lot of times candy wrappers got stuck there or pieces of paper too big for the hose. He reached down and caught something between his fingers.

It was a credit card receipt from a gas station.

He laid it on the dashboard and got on his knees so he could see if there were any more.

He ran his hand under the springs but did not feel anything. When he got up he lifted the floormat and found a crushed dirt clod, some loose pine needles and another receipt under the edge. This one was a hotel bill. He set it on the dashboard, too.

Mr. Ellsworth wanted a trophy wife, someone he could show off to his business friends. The rest of the time she was supposed to be happy with what she had, which was a lot. But she was a smart woman. She needed a life of her own. That was why they started growing apart. At least Mr. Ellsworth had tried to do something about it. Paulino remembered how happy she was last Monday. She could not stop talking about the weekend getaway, just the two of them, like a second honeymoon. When he had to cancel she must have been sad.

Paulino saw the address at the top of the hotel bill.

It was from the Doubletree Lodge at Triangle Lake.

The other receipt was from a Union 76 station on Highway 5, just north of L.A.

That was on the way.

If they took the trip, after all, why didn't Mr. Ellsworth want him to know?

Paulino tried to put it out of his mind. It was none of his business. He placed the receipts in the glovebox, then went around to the other side.

As he opened the passenger door he noticed some streaks on the inside of the window. He imagined Mrs. Ellsworth falling asleep last night, on the way home from the lake, with her face against the glass. It looked like she had put her hand there, too, to support her head. He placed his fingers over the streaks.

Then he remembered that there had not been a trip.

That was what Mr. Ellsworth said.

Paulino decided to roll the window down into the door before wiping it. That way the rubber seal would do some of the work for him, like a squeegee. He turned the key and hit the button. But when the window came back up one of her lacquered fingernails came with it, wedged halfway under the seal. And the streaks were worse, with a pink rainbow clinging to them, as if the gears inside the door were wet with strawberry soda.

A faint purple residue came off on his blue towel.

Something had spattered or spilled against the window, a soft drink, maybe. And she had tried to wipe it off and broken her nail. The litter bag under the glovebox held a few crumpled tissues. Paulino emptied it and saw stains on the tissues that had dried to a darker color, like dirty lipstick.

He probed under the seat with the vacuum. As soon as he did that something hard started to rattle. It was not a piece of paper. This time there was a long, pointed object, rounded at one end, stuck between the floormat and the door. He plucked it from the nozzle and looked at it.

One of Mrs. Ellsworth's high heels.

The rubber tip had cut a sharp black line into the mat. The line continued out of the passenger compartment and left a gouge in the paint, just inside the door, before the heel snapped off.

If she was asleep Mr. Ellsworth must have carried her out of the car. But he had not lifted her legs. It was more like he had dragged her. The edge of the mat was curled where her shoe had snagged it.

He pulled on the mat, and the rubberized backing made a sucking sound as it peeled away. The carpet underneath was wet. He dropped the mat on the asphalt and looked at his fingers.

They were red.

Suddenly a breeze came up and blew through the open doors. He felt it in his chest and in his fingers as he waited for them to dry. He tried wiping them on the towel but they were still sticky.

Now there was an emptiness in his stomach,

as if he had skipped breakfast and the coffee was ready to pass out of his body in a rush. He wished it were time for lunch but he had hours, long hours, ahead of him. He looked around at the car wash where he worked, where everything was made clean and spotless again and no one had to think about what happened in the world outside. He heard the grinding of the machinery and the hiss of the spray, saw the scum on the water as it ran down to the sewer and the steam rising into the polluted sky, and knew that even this place was not safe anymore.

The street was packed with cars, dirty inside and out, pumping so much filth into the air that the sky might never open again. It was too soon to pick up Rosalie, and if he tried to drive home in the morning rush he could lose his way and be trapped out there forever.

He saw the rest of the crew, wiping and polishing for tips, joking and staying busy so they would not have to look at what was on their towels, as the laundry barrel filled up until it would be too heavy to lift at the end of the day. He saw the customers, reading newspapers and making cell phone calls and staring at nothing, waiting to be born again, fresh and squeaky-clean. And he saw Mr. Ellsworth, watching him.

The man came over and stood next to the mat with its sticky underside turned up.

"What do you want me to do with this?" said Paulino.

"Throw it away."

"Why?"

"I'll get new ones."

"But why?"

"Because they're ruined."

Paulino knew he should not say anything else but could not stop himself. "How's Mrs. Ellsworth?"

The man squinted at him.

"She went away."

"Where?"

"To visit her relatives. She won't be back for a long time." He took out his wallet and handed over another hundred dollar bill. "Here. For the mats."

"We don't have any," said Paulino.

"Get some."

"You have to go to the dealer for that."

"You do it for me." He tried to give him fifty more. "Keep the change."

Paulino got out of the car.

"Where are you going? You're not finished . . ."

He went over to Ruben, who was working on a Sportage at the end of the ramp.

"I can pay you twenty today," Ruben said.

"Forget about it, *vato*." Paulino took the first

hundred from his pocket and handed him both bills.

"What's this for?"

"The LX420."

"Huh?"

"If you don't want to do it, that's okay with me. Give some to Craig and Manny. And Linda. She works hard, too."

Paulie walked on to his Escort at the back of the lot. He took off his jumpsuit as he went, stepped out of it and left it on the asphalt without breaking stride. Then he got behind the wheel and turned the key.

He pulled into the alley and squeezed past the line of waiting cars, hoping to spot a sidestreet that was clear. On the way to find Rosalie he turned on his radio to block out the traffic noise. The first station he came to was playing power oldies. He raised the volume and began to sing along, not paying attention to the words. After a mile or so he realized it was the same tune he had heard when he woke up this morning, a love song that kept circling back on itself and starting again. *You make me feel so brand-new*, sang Al Green's high, soulful voice. *Let's stay together, whether times are good or bad or happy or sad* . . . The lyrics sounded so beautiful to Paulino that his eyes burned. He kept singing along even after the record was over. He did not want it to end.

The Dead Cop

Standing in the red glow, Decker watched a pattern emerge at the center of the paper. It appeared to be a horizon broken by several jagged vertical lines. A few seconds more and the lines sharpened into what might be swords or spears. He waited for something else to take form, anything at all that might provide a clue, but there were no surrounding details in this frame, either. And it was impossible to remember exactly what he had caught in his viewfinder that night.

As he leaned over the tray, squinting in the metallic fumes, he heard a ringing. He reached for the timer, then realized he had not bothered to set it for this print. The ringing came again,

Dennis Etchison

a faint chirping, as if a small bird had found its way into his studio on the other side of the thin wall. He slid the sheet of paper into the stop bath and opened the door, flooding the dark-room with light from the overhead windows. It was no good, anyway; the pattern had come up too fast and was already turning black.

His telephone rang again.

"Hello?"

"Pete? Thank God."

"Hi, honey." The glare from the panes in the skylight blinded him. "What's wrong?"

"Nothing. I mean—I was about to hang up. I thought you'd left."

"Not yet."

"Are you okay?"

"Sure."

"You sound so far away."

He turned the receiver so the mouthpiece was closer to his lips. The stubble on his chin caught in the tiny holes, magnifying what sounded like a scraping in his ear. "I was in the darkroom."

"Oh, sorry."

"That's all right. I'm finished."

"You are? Well, tell me!"

"Tell you what?"

"How did it go?"

The bare white walls took on texture, first the rows of dark rectangles, favorite enlargements he had mounted for display over the years, then the corkboard filled with test prints from his new assignment: closeups of burgers and fries and soft drinks in cups, all suspended in space on a folded paper swing. The pale yellow fries fanned out from their container like the severed fingers of children caught in the mouth of a cornucopia.

"The job? It went fine."

"Really?"

"I had trouble with the Monster Gulp. The ice melted, but the guy from the Feed Bag wanted to be sure it looked cold. So I had to spray the cup. The water kept beading up and running off. I tried mineral water and corn syrup, and I finally got it."

"Congratulations!"

"They still have to see the proofs. Everything is supposed to be high-key. Bigger than life."

"I'm so proud of you! So—what were you doing? When I called, I mean. You said you were in the darkroom."

"Just cleaning up."

"Oh." She paused, as if allowing for a delay in the phone lines. "So you can go home now. Unless you have—something else to work on."

"No."

She sighed, a white hissing like steam released inside the plastic earpiece. "That's good. I mean, I'll see you at home, then."

"Okay."

The conversation did not seem to be over. He waited.

"Oh," she said, "I almost forgot. The shoe repair, on Pico. They have my Ferragamos. Could you stop by? He closes at six."

"I thought you get off at five."

"It's Counselors' Night. I have to stay till seven-thirty."

His throat tensed. "It'll be dark by then."

"We have a lighted parking lot. It's safe. I promise."

He didn't say anything.

"Are you okay?" she said.

"Sure. I'll get the shoes. Don't worry about it."

"Thanks. You may as well go ahead and eat. There's half a barbecued chicken left."

"Okay. Or I'll pick up something on the way."

"The Apple Pan?" she said.

"Maybe the Feed Bag. I could strap on a burger."

She laughed.

"Be careful, Cory," he said, very seriously.

"You, too."

"I feel fine now. Honest."

"I *know* you do," she said with an unnatural emphasis.

"Love you."

"Me, too," he said, and hung up.

He looked at his watch. It was only a little after five. If he worked fast he could print one more frame from the night club. He would need as much contrast as possible to hold the details; #6 paper, full-strength developer, and maybe some dodging. But there was still time.

When he turned out of the parking lot onto Venice Boulevard, the traffic was bumper-to-bumper. A diffused glaze hung over the cars and trucks pointing east; in the opposite direction the light was more intense, as though bounced off aluminized reflectors somewhere above the haze while the sun prepared to sink into the ocean several miles to the west. He joined the flow eastward, but only for a few blocks. At the first corner, a crowd of Hispanic workers gathered under the American shield of the old Helms Bakery building, waiting with bowed heads for buses that would take them deeper into the city. He tried not to look at them as he inched forward to La Cienega, where he finally made a left, heading home.

The route was a relentless grind at this time of day, jammed with workers on their way back to Washington and Jefferson and the ghettos of South Central. Eyes shone white and fixed behind dirty windshields as large hands gripped steering wheels with grim determination. He moved over for another left at Pico so he could stop by the shoe repair shop. Then he noticed that it was already after six.

He had taken too long with the last batch of prints. There was nothing usable in the envelope; but it was important to be sure. A promise was a promise, especially to his son. He would tell his wife that he had spotted some flaw in the proofs for the Feed Bag and decided to do them over. As for Gary's pictures, at least he had tried. He hoped the boy would understand.

Beneath the Santa Monica freeway, the hard bass rhythms of gangsta rap shook his Mercedes, reverberating in the underpass like the aftershocks of a temblor. He should have taken Robertson. There was nothing to do about it now. He rolled his window up tightly and waited for the traffic to move again.

Another tense mile and the pale, white-gold lettering of the Great Western Bank building wavered into view through the mist. Now the letters spelled out the name of the new owner, a publisher whose sexually graphic magazines sold so well that he had bought the property outright. Years ago, when John Wayne served as the bank's television spokesman, a larger-than-life bronze statue of the late actor on horseback was erected by the entrance, like a sentinel protecting the Westside from attack by outsiders. The statue was still there. What would the conservative cowboy think, knowing that he now guarded an upwardly-mobile pornographer's beachhead on the corner of La Cienega and Wilshire, inside the once secure boundaries of Beverly Hills?

He drove Wilshire to Rodeo, a street lined with the world's most expensive shops, some so exclusive that they required advance credit approval before granting admission. An Asian couple left Gucci's and crossed in front of Decker's car, unaware that jaywalking was a crime in this city, while groups of young men and women with unfamiliar brand names on their jeans strolled past Fendi and Van Cleef & Arpel's, their European accents sounding oddly appropriate amid the many foreign-owned businesses here. The tourist section was only a few blocks long, but he found himself stuck behind a Grey Line bus that paused at every storefront in order to give its passengers a chance to focus their cameras through the tinted windows. By the time he came to Sunset Boulevard the lights of the Beverly Hills Hotel were on, throwing smudged shadows of tall palm trees across the pastel facade. Now, this close to home, he should have begun to unwind. But there was something about the shadows that held his attention and would not let go. He tried to ignore the angular verticals against the uneven horizon as he waited for the line of taillights to make their turns, then continued across and up into Beaumont Canyon.

Dennis Etchison

The last mile was the hardest. After only a few days off work he was shocked to find traffic in the canyon dramatically worse, with so many trucks and oversized sport utility vehicles that he could see no more than a single car length ahead. It took twenty minutes to creep a few hundred yards. In front of him a Mexican gardener's pickup groaned and shuddered, brakes squealing every ten feet. An Isuzu Trooper rode his bumper, its elevated headlights burning holes in his rearview mirror, then began to honk. Other vehicles took up the call until the canyon sounded like New York City at high noon. When a Range Rover cut out of line and tried a J-turn at the first cross street, downhill drivers flashed their high beams and made obscene gestures, only their thrusting fingers visible in the glare. Decker thought he heard the crunch of a fender somewhere ahead, followed by angry voices, and for the next several minutes all movement ceased. The Trooper boiled over in front of a mansion protected by an electrified fence, the gardener's pickup vibrated as it lurched and rolled backward, dropping leaves and clods of dirt onto Decker's hood. He cleaned his windshield with a few passes of the wipers. As the blades came to rest, he noticed a police car parked at the side of the road.

How did it get here so fast? he wondered. He saw no sign of a wreck, no broken glass. Perhaps there had not been an accident and the mere sight of the police car had caused the slowdown, its very presence a deterrent. He thought of giving the officer a wave and a smile, but the patrol car's windows were dark and misted over. He drove on past.

By the time he got home it was after eight o'clock. Cory was not there yet.

When he called her school there was no answer. He told himself that she was probably stuck in traffic on the other side of the hill.

He sat down at the kitchen table and opened the envelope.

With such badly underexposed negatives there was not much to see in the prints, despite his best efforts to retain an image. Even on high-contrast paper the frames had gone black with almost nothing in the shadows. The dodging left an opaque halo at the center, ghostly against the surrounding darkness.

He would tell Gary that he had screwed up. It was embarrassing. The boy had only asked him to take a few publicity photos of the concert. That was easy enough. But something had gone wrong.

He tried to remember.

Somehow, in the noise and the crush of

bodies, he had loaded his Leica with a slower portrait film instead of Tri-X. When he discovered his mistake later, he pushed it as far as he dared in the darkroom, but all that gave him was a series of exposures with severely blocked-up highlights and the remaining areas unprintably thin. They might make for some interesting abstract blowups, something that would work in a gallery show, but that was not what his son wanted. It was a shame; the night had been special. The word was that there were important people in the audience, people whose opinions could decide the band's future. So they had gone for it, jamming retro Goth at an earsplitting level, amps cranked up to the point where dogs howl and chase their tails, Gary's fingers raking the metal strings until what looked like drops of blood flew from the guitar, as the air grew heavy and began to crackle like an electrical storm. A performance that would never come again. And Decker had blown it.

He studied the prints one last time.

There was the name of his son's band under the ceiling, the letters an unreadable snowstorm of grain in the spotlights. Below, Gary and Mark and the rest of the group were only blurred shadows. Then the false horizon line that was the edge of the stage, and below that blackness. Decker remembered the audience rushing forward in a dark wave, pressing closer. They must have had their arms raised, because there were the vertical lines again, extending up from the bottom half of the frame.

He got out his magnifying glass.

Now he saw rounded silhouettes rising out of the darkness—closed fists, cheering the band on. But what were the lines *above* the hands? Though it had happened only a week ago, he had trouble remembering. The lines were so sharp they could be horns or the ears of wild animals.

He would have to ask Gary.

He picked up the phone, started to dial his son's number. He'd tell him that the pictures were no good, but maybe there was another gig coming up soon. And the next time he'd get it right.

Wait.

This was Thursday. Gary would be rehearsing. Where? At Mark's, just like every Tuesday and Thursday since junior high. He was probably there now. Decker carried the cordless phone to the living room and flicked on the lamp as he dialed Mark's number.

"Hello, this is the Fordham residence . . ."

"Hi, Jack." Why was the lamp so dim? He found the remote, turned on the TV. "Are Mark and Gary—?"

"No one can come to the phone, but if you'd care to leave a message, we'll return your call as soon as possible." Decker broke the connection.

He poured himself an inch of Scotch. On-screen, a sitcom about a minority family was in progress. The program had just started but the members of the family were already trading insults like a neighborhood gang playing the dozens. He kept the sound low and sat down on the sofa.

Maybe Gary and Mark were over at the new drummer's. What was his name? Cory would know. He'd ask her, as soon as she got home. He took a sip of the Scotch and tried to relax while he waited.

Seated under the lamp, he felt detached from the rest of the room, as though it were receding even as he gazed across it, at the carpet and furniture and the photographs mounted in windowbox frames along the walls. There was the one of Cory by candlelight, then Cory and little Gary waving by the tree in the yard, Gary playing his first guitar, Gary's high school graduation. Their faces smiled back as always from the richly gradated prints, but now his own technique began to irritate him. The background areas in each image were so dark that in this light the faces appeared to be no more than pale reflections, as if he had forgotten to fix them in acid and they were now fading to black, about to disappear. Only the television family shone clearly out of the shadows, striking obvious poses and waiting for laughs from an unseen audience. Then the program dissolved to a series of commercials.

He focused on the screen as images flickered across it, products so brightly lighted that they seemed more alive than anything else in the room. He wondered if there would be a spot for the Feed Bag, its oozing burgers and fries supported by disposable cardboard neck trays, as he had shot them for the layout this morning. But it was too soon; the drive-thru chain had only just opened, with L.A. as the first test market. Soon his photographs would pop up on billboards all over the city and he would have more assignments than he could handle. It was good to be working again. He felt as if he had taken off much more than a week.

He drained the Scotch and got up to pour another, as a live teaser for the evening news came on. There were unconfirmed reports of another drive-by shooting. A special Eyeball Report on gang violence was promised at eleven.

Where did it happen this time? Decker wondered.

He thought uneasily of Cory and her class in the East Valley, an area known for gang activity. And tonight she had stayed late for a meeting there. He imagined his wife on the way to her car, after. Then other cars, low-riders, cruising into the empty lot and calling out, taunting her, and the doors flying open, the weapons in their dirty hands, the tight-lipped smiles and the cat-calls and their brown eyes turning black as a single weak security light flickered by the back of the building . . .

It was another two-and-a-half hours till the newscast.

As he picked up the phone to call the school again, headlights flashed outside and a tall, pointed shadow fell across the windows. He hurried to the front door in time to see a car pass on the lane, the silhouette of the old pine tree sweeping the front of the house. Then there was only the darkness. He went back inside.

He decided to try the police. He punched 911 and got a busy signal. He pressed redial, as someone opened the back door.

"Cory?"

In the kitchen, she stumbled and almost fell as she stepped over the threshhold. Her books and papers flapped to the floor. He ignored them and held her, gripping her arms.

"Hey," she said, "take it easy . . ."

"Are you all right?"

"Of course I am. You're hurting me. Pete . . ."

He hugged her.

"Hi," she said.

He let her go. "Hi."

"Sorry I'm late. You wouldn't believe how many parents showed up. Have you been home long?"

He took a deep breath. "No."

"Did you eat?"

"Not yet."

"You're supposed to eat, remember?"

"I was waiting for you."

"I couldn't help it, Pete!"

"It's all right."

"Well, I guess I can make us something. Just let me get out of these shoes . . ."

"I'm not very hungry."

"Did you get my new heels?"

"I didn't have time. The traffic was unbelievable."

She walked through to the living room, taking off her coat.

"Well, I'll just have to get them on the way to work. If he's open that early . . ."

"I was thinking. Maybe you should quit, Cory. It's not like we need the money."

"It's not about the money."

"What *is* it about?"

"Those kids. It matters to them."

"Does it?"

"Why?" she snapped. "Because they're Chicanos?"

"That's not what I mean."

"What *do* you mean?"

227

He backed off and sank onto the couch. "I was worried, that's all."

She turned to him, one side of her face in shadow.

"You don't have to," she said gently. "Please." She came over and stood before the couch. Now her features were lost completely to the backlight, only a few sharp strands of her hair outlined against the lamp. "We're doing fine. You're back at work, and so am I. It's better this way. Isn't it?"

He took her hand and drew her down next to him. Cory was naive but she meant well. Over her shoulder, he saw the TV family collapse together onto their sofa, convulsed with laughter, knowing that their day was coming. At least it was not here yet.

"Sure," he said.

"There. See? So what are we talking about?"

Outside, at the end of the lane, the rush-hour traffic in the canyon had ended. A lone car with a broken muffler sped toward Mulholland, radial tires screaming around the hairpin curves.

"I tried to get to Pico," he said, "but it's like a war zone out there."

"I know. Ever since they closed the Sepulveda Pass."

"When did they do that?"

She looked at him peculiarly. "It's been awhile."

"Oh."

She lowered her head and squeezed his hand.

"At least we've got a traffic cop now," he said.

"Do we?" she said distantly.

"He was parked by Tremont Road. I passed him on the way up. I hope it does some good."

"I hope so, too." She studied his eyes. Then she said, "Hey, when do I get to see the pictures?"

She meant the Feed Bag layout. Of course. "It's only burgers and fries. Not exactly art."

"Well, I'm proud of you, anyway. You know that, don't you?"

He put his arm around her shoulders and drew her close. He felt her cold skin and her warm breath against the side of his neck. They sat that way for a minute.

"I was wondering," he said. "What was that drummer's name?"

She pulled away. "What drummer?"

"In Gary's band. The new one."

"What are you talking about?"

"I thought I'd give him a call. Do you have the number?"

"No, Pete," she said after a long pause. "I don't."

She stood abruptly and went into the kitchen. He wondered if there was trouble in the band, possibly a falling out that he did not know about. For the moment he decided not to pursue it. He heard her open the refrigerator and set something heavy on the table. Then it was quiet. Another TV program began, the latest installment of *Unanswered Questions*. Tonight's episode was about the recently-discovered missing pages from the diary of a dead film actress. The pages purportedly contained the solution to an unsolved murder. Decker found the remote control and raised the volume, as Cory said something unintelligible.

From the kitchen doorway he saw her seated at the table, the leftover barbecued chicken now in a Pyrex dish, and next to that the photos from the concert. She had removed them from the envelope.

"What are these?" she said.

"Nothing."

"I asked you a question, Peter."

He started toward her. "Please, don't look at them."

"Why not?"

"They're from Gary's last concert. At the Box Club. But they didn't come out."

"Then," she said, "what are you going to do with them?"

He took the photos from her and slipped them back into the envelope. "Burn them, I guess."

"Good."

She turned away and began making the dinner.

They hardly spoke for the rest of the evening. When the eleven o'clock news came on, she was already asleep. He sat up and watched the report about the drive-by shooting. Witnesses claimed it had happened in South Gate, miles from here, but no body had been found yet. In bed he listened to her breathing next to him and thought about her job in the Valley, where conditions were just as bad. The Chief of Police called it an isolated incident but he had taken the precaution of ordering a tactical alert throughout the city. That means it's spreading, thought Decker. He fell asleep dreaming of a parking lot very much like the one behind her school, or what he imagined it to be like. Something was going on there, but he could not see what it was through the fog.

In the morning he had a meeting at the ad agency. Fortunately it was not until eleven o'clock, well after the rush hour. On the way down the hill he tuned to the classical music station, but FM reception here was so weak that the strings sounded like keys scraping the side of his car. He switched to the AM band for the news. There was a late-breaking story about another disturbance, this time in the Crenshaw district. They were getting closer.

Dennis Etchison

He was relieved to see another squad car on Beaumont. It was parked in roughly the same location as the one last night, between Tremont and Huffington Place. The motor was off and the tinted windows were rolled up so that once again he could not see the officer inside. But it was good to know that the LAPD had finally heeded the Westside's pleas for more protection. The canyons were especially vulnerable, with the Valley to the north and the rest of the L.A. basin to the south, not to mention the Mexican border beyond.

The meeting went smoothly. The rep from the Feed Bag wanted more light and color in the photos. That would be easy enough; it was simply a matter of printing them up. Decker explained that losing the shadows would mean less depth and realism, but apparently they wanted their product to appear two-dimensional, with nothing left to draw the eye beyond the surface of the picture. No problem, he told them. He knew that he could do it in an afternoon. He also knew that he would put it off as long as possible, now that the job had become even less interesting.

He came home early enough to beat the worst of the traffic, though more than a few commuters were already starting their trek up and over the hill. He passed the electrified fence where the Trooper had overheated last night; the man-

sion was guarded by an iron servant with out-stretched hand, its enameled face painted an innacurate but politically correct pink. A zippy young businessmen with cell phone drifted over the line in his BMW, a divorcée chauffeured her blond daughters in an aging Rolls Royce, a private shuttle full of tourists turned up a side-street in search of movie star homes. At the first big curve the traffic slowed to a second-gear crawl. Now, at this time of day, he realized how many nonresidents used the canyon as a free-way alternate. Ahead he saw plumbers and electricians in company vans, day laborers in rusty Fords and Chevies, college students in un-washed Toyotas and Nissans, teenagers cruis-ing in ragged convertibles and four-wheel drives. He was sure that none of them were from around here.

When he got home he watched the early news. A local reporter was at the site of the lat-est incident. In the background, gang members in knit caps and baggy clothes mugged for the camera with raised fists, some making the sign of the horns with their fingers.

He called his son's number, but there was no answer.

In the evening, *Unanswered Questions* pre-sented Part Two of its story about the late ac-tress's secret diary. The missing pages had turned up in an estate sale at a home once owned by an actor who died of alcoholism years ago.

Decker spent the next hour searching his house for the blow-ups from the concert, and finally decided that Cory must have thrown them out.

Perhaps there was a problem between her and the boy, something that she had kept from him. Why was she angry? He knew better than to press her on the subject. She would tell him in her own time. Meanwhile, he would let the problem work itself out, whatever it was. The prints were not that important, as long as he had the negatives.

A teaser for the Eyeball News promised more coverage of the unrest, which appeared to be escalating. Shots from several live remotes around the city featured interviews with spokesmen for various gangs, including blacks, Hispanics, Koreans, even a few tattooed skin-heads.

He realized that Cory had not come home yet. It was late enough for him to feel uncomfortable but too early to panic. There was no point in calling the school with the switchboard closed. He could go there and try to find her, but what if she was already on her way?

Now there were unconfirmed reports of more trouble, including a firebombing in Culver City, only a mile or so from his studio.

He couldn't just sit here.

He left a note for her on the back door.

A mist had moved down from Mulholland and into the canyon. The houses were milky and indistinct behind the trees, cars glistening and silvered in the driveways. Diffused headlights swung past like lanterns in fog. He was surprised to see that the police car was still here. As far as he could tell it had not moved. For the first time he wondered if it might be a movie prop, with location shoots so common in this area. He slowed down, pausing at the curb for a better look.

The shield on the side appeared to be authentic, down to the seal of the city of Los Angeles. If it was a fake it was perfect. Too perfect. But if it was the real thing, why would the LAPD leave one of their cars in the same spot for days on end?

He tuned to an all-news station as he left the canyon. A ten o'clock curfew had just been declared for much of greater L.A. Decker glanced at the dashboard clock and decided there was time.

He took Beverly Glen to Pico, turned right at 20th Century-Fox and continued up Motor. The Cheviot Hills Tennis Center was dark except for a pair of white shorts and a disembodied arm swinging a racket through the mist. The neon sign for D. B. Cooper's glowed like faint landing lights near National, and then the mist cleared and he made out the tall water tower that had always reminded him of a Martian spacecraft standing above the old MGM backlot, now owned by Sony.

If there had been a fire anywhere nearby there was no sign of it now. At the corner of Motor and Venice, two patrol cars blocked off the parking lot of the Versailles Cuban Restaurant while officers stood by the exit, checking ID's. As he approached the Helms Bakery building he slowed, preparing to turn into the tenants' lot, and discovered that the sidestreet was barricaded. An officer in a riot helmet waved him on, his eyes hidden behind the protective visor.

The next news bulletin announced a bombing in the garment district, near downtown L.A.

That was where Gary had his loft.

The horizon to the east swirled with mist heavy enough to be smoke. Decker wished for a car phone so that he could warn his son. Where was the nearest telephone booth? The gas stations at Roberston and at La Cienega were closed off with wooden sawhorses and the fast food restaurants up and down Venice had all shut down early.

He would have to drive there.

But the entrance ramp to the I-10 was

blocked by more barricades. The surface streets between here and the dark heart of the city would be unpredictable. Olympic passed directly through Koreatown, and every other major east-west artery intersected at least one ethnic stronghold. La Cienega was already closed to the south, in the direction of Washington and Jefferson and the black neighborhoods. Soon the western section would be cut off on all sides, effectively isolated.

Had Gary tried to call?

Cory would know.

If she had made it home.

He cut back up National to Pico, heading north. The mist thickened again and he had to use his wipers, sweeping away what appeared to be fine ash as well as moisture. As he neared Sunset the traffic grew congested. Beverly Glen, Benedict and Beaumont Canyons were all freeway alternates and late commuters now searched for any route still open to the Valley. Through the glass he heard blips of competing radio stations in other cars, each with a different version of the news. There had been a minor disturbance or a full-scale riot in East L.A. or Watts, with no serious injuries, mounting casualties or dozens dead. The police had the situation contained or the city was under seige and the Mayor had called for the National

Guard. He kept his window closed and his door locked.

He knew now that he was on his own. They all were. L.A. was not a city but a freeway system that mixed together tribes with nothing in common except an overlapping geography, directed and distributed by the grid. That was why the traffic was out of control wherever people crossed each other's turf. They had no sense of community, no respect for the routes they were forced to share, and everything not part of one's neighborhood was enemy territory, a no man's land to be trashed. Decker finally understood the appeal of sport utility vehicles. With their high cabs and reinforced bodies, they were like tanks ready for the battlefield. He pounded the wheel and leaned on the horn.

Halfway up the canyon he found himself idling next to the abandoned police car. He wondered if it belonged to an officer who lived on this street, or one who came here at all hours for private reasons, perhaps to visit a girlfriend. Now, against the line of descending headlights, he thought he saw someone in the driver's seat. The head was cocked at an odd angle, as if the officer were sleeping it off. But before he could get a closer look, there was a break in the bottleneck and the traffic began to move again.

*　　*　　*

Cory's car was parked in back but the house was dark. He rushed through to the living room and found her waiting by the sofa in the light of the television set. She threw her arms around his neck and clung to him. He kissed her as an Eyeball News reporter conducted a live interview. Onscreen, firefighters picked through the charred remains of a convenience store, while round-eyed children with dirty fingers waved at the camera from behind police barricades.

"I'm sorry," she said. She felt his face carefully with her hands, as if he were fragile. "I had to stay with the children. Nobody could get through, not even the buses."

Over her shoulder, the TV coverage continued.

"What's happened?" he said.

"They're still looking for the body. The Crips say it's in Watts. The Brown Brotherhood says East L.A. So far, it's just a rumor. But all the gangs are taking credit."

"Why?"

"It was a cop. At least that's what they say. It's just an excuse to loot and burn. I go to work every day so the children will have a chance, and now they're destroying their own neighborhoods! It's stupid, so stupid . . ."

"They know what they're doing."

"What do you mean?"

"They want the city, this time."

Her eyes were enormous in the semidarkness. "That doesn't make sense."

"Doesn't it?" He had hoped she would see the handwriting on the wall, but apparently she did not, even now. He started for the kitchen. "Did Gary call?"

She did not answer.

He turned on the kitchen light, looking for the phone. "He might be trying to get us. I tried, but there's never any answer. What did he do, change the number?"

Behind him, he heard her make a sound in her throat. When he turned around her eyes were full of tears.

"Oh, God," she said.

"What's wrong? Did something happen to Gary?"

She regained control of herself and went to him. "I thought you were all right. But you're not. Jack Fordham's been getting calls. He said it was a prank . . ."

"Tell me, Cory."

He attempted to push her away but her hands tightened, forcing him to look at her.

"We'll be okay," she said. "You'll see. I'll take care of you . . ."

"Tell me!"

"You've been sick. You don't remember the last year, not anything at all, do you?"

"It's been a week, Cory. I've been off work for a week!"

"Pete, I want you to listen to me."

He felt strangely calm. He knew what she was going to say, as if he had heard it before, in a dream. He saw the pictures in his mind again, of the parking lot and the gang, the confrontation. It was not about Cory, after all.

"Honey, Gary's dead."

No, he thought, not yet. Somehow she knew what he had been dreaming. But that did not mean it had to happen. There was still time to stop it, to get the boy out of there before it was too late.

"You're lying," he said.

He went outside and started the Mercedes, dropped into gear and clicked on the headlights. He wiped a clear spot on the fogged windshield and rolled forward over wet leaves, low branches slapping the glass. For a moment all he could see was a wall of mist. Then he heard a scream. He looked at the rearview mirror. A shadow reached out to the car, red in the glow of the taillights.

He unlocked the passenger door.

"Are you coming or not?" he shouted.

She stood there, her face crawling with rivulets of water, then got in.

The canyon was empty of traffic as far as he could see. The mist that had collected in the hills now poured down like smoke, heavy with moisture, a glittering whiteness that his head-lights could not penetrate. He turned right, to-ward Sunset and the city.

"Will you tell me where we're going?"

He ignored her. Even with the defroster on the windshield did not stay clear. Beads of moisture began to collect on the inside of the glass as he leaned forward, following the double line. The fog thinned briefly and he saw the lights of houses twinkling behind the trees. Then the white wall closed around the car and he was driving blind again. He pressed harder on the accelerator. With visibility so limited he felt alert to any possibility. The familiar land-marks would only have lulled him into an illu-sion of security, leaving him more vulnerable. That was the danger of believing in surfaces, in what showed. Now, aware of how much he could not see, he was ready for anything. It was more than an esthetic preference. It was a mat-ter of survival.

"Please," she said, "where—?"

"To get Gary." He felt her shocked eyes on him, heard the sharp intake of breath above the pulse of the wipers. "If you can't handle that, get out now."

"I thought it was good that you forgot every-thing," she said softly, "but now . . ."

A car passed them, speeding downhill from Mulholland.

"At least let me drive!"

He knew she was trying to trick him so that she could turn around and go home. The tires hissed over the wet pavement, trees sagged and waved in front of lampposts. Somewhere above the fog great wings flapped, marking the pace. Then the fog blew aside, like curtains parting on a stage, and in the spotlight he saw the police car.

She opened her window and leaned out, signaling for help. He pulled her roughly back into the seat.

"Forget it," he told her. "There's never anybody in that car."

The flapping became a roar. The sky grew brighter and the fog blew aside, as a helicopter hovered overhead with its searchlight trained on the abandoned car.

As they pulled abreast of it he saw again the form inside, illuminated clearly now in the circle of light from above. There was a head and shoulders, leaning precariously to one side in the seat, about to topple over.

Not even the Westside is safe, he thought. They must have killed him right here, in Bel Air, but we were all too busy to notice.

"There's your dead cop," he said. "They don't know where he is? Well, they do now!"

He climbed out of the Mercedes and raised his face to the light, holding his arms up.

"Here!"

She ran to him and dragged him over to the police car, digging her fingers into his hair to make him see what was inside. It was a department-store mannequin dressed in a uniform with badge and hat, propped up behind the wheel. She shouted in his ear as the blades sliced the air.

"Look, Pete, it's only a dummy! For traffic control! They call it passive law enforcement . . . !"

She was right, but what did that matter? Someone had seen it, one of the cars passing through, a gardener or a workman or a transient, and the rumors had started.

No cars had passed them going uphill. Did that mean Sunset was blocked off?

He hoped so. Because the gang would come back, the ones who had done it, to show the way so others would know who was to lead them. Then they would all come, from Compton and Inglewood and Huntington Park and South Gate, from Monterey Park and El Sereno and Silverlake and Little Saigon, swarming across the basin in a united front, a tide that would sweep away everything in its path. They had been sitting tight in their ghettos, waiting for someone to fire the opening shot so they could move in force. For years they had hit and run with small strikes, a convenience store, a mall, even picking off members of rival gangs, feeding on each other as the frustration grew. Now all that was over. Their time had come at last.

The helicopter banked and rose higher, flapping away.

"Come home with me, Pete," he heard her say in the sudden silence.

"Who killed my son?"

"He was my son, too. It doesn't matter now. It's over . . ."

"You're wrong," he said.

He squinted, struggling to see the details, as the mist returned. He had captured a piece of it in his viewfinder that night, just before it started . . .

Under the track lights was a banner with the name of his son's band, and below that the blur that he knew to be Gary on lead guitar. Then the horizon line of the stage, the heads of the crowd, and the thrusting verticals. He stared into the swirling particles of fog as if studying the grain pattern in a frame of film, and this time he refused to look away until he saw it all.

The pattern began to move.

Beyond the edges of the frame were bouncing heads, the bare-chested boys with shirts tied around their waists. The music assaulted his eardrums so that he had to shut his eyes but the image remained clear.

There, in the middle of the crowd, several figures were not moving to the music. They had slipped past the security guards after the set started and made their way down front. He had no trouble spotting them because they were wearing jackets with emblems on the back, their colors. He felt bodies pressing closer and hot breath on his neck, and realized that Cory was clinging to him.

He lowered the camera long enough to free himself from her. The night air chilled him. He opened his eyes and saw her standing in front of him, about to disappear into the mist.

"The name," he said. "What was the name of Gary's band?"

"Please . . ."

"Say it!"

"The New Goths," she told him, and began to cry again.

Yes, he thought, that's it. The same as the emblem on the jackets. They came to the club to see who had stolen their name. That was why the weapons came out, at first only a few thin, jagged lines in his viewfinder, as still as swords at rest. When the song ended they put them away and did not take them out again until the parking lot. They were the last things Decker saw that night, the last things Gary ever saw.

Now the fog behind Cory became white, so bright that the outline of her body seemed a part of it. He saw her disembodied head turning to look behind her, as the helicopter reappeared above the horizon at the top of the canyon. The blades beat the air and the fog cleared and he saw the jagged lines of dead trees and the legs of a water tower against the sky, and then the rounded shapes of heads rising up in the beam of the searchlight.

"They forgot," he said.

She turned back to him, confused.

He thought of how Beaumont Canyon continued on up to Mulholland and then all the way down the hill to the Valley on the other side, to Panorama City and Pacoima and San Fernando and the gang enclaves there.

"They stopped them at Sunset," he told her. "But they forgot about Mulholland."

"What . . . ?"

"It's too late now," he said. "They're here."

They came marching down the hill, ignoring the police helicopter. He saw the blond stubble of their hair shining in the searchlight and the swastikas tattooed on their skulls, and he knew that it was not the Crips or the Bloods or the New Goths, not this time. They were skinheads, whatever they called themselves.

The helicopter boomed a warning but they kept coming, the lines of their sharp, splintered

Dennis Etchison

baseball bats held high. Their eyes shone like the eyes of wild animals, like raccoon eyes, yellow and terrible. When they saw Decker and his wife and the Mercedes they started running and yelling.

He pushed her behind him and stood his ground, stepping out into the center of the pavement to meet them.

Inside The Cackle Factory

Uncle Miltie did not look very happy. Someone had left a half-smoked cigar on his head, and now the wrapper began to come unglued in the rain. A few seconds more and dark stains dripped over his slick hair, ran down his cheeks and collected in his open mouth, the bits of chewed tobacco clinging like wet sawdust to a beaver's front teeth.

"Time," announced Marty, clicking his stopwatch.

Lisa Anne tried to get his attention from across the room, but it was too late. She saw him note the hour and minute on his clipboard.

"Please pass your papers to the right," he said, "and one of our monitors will pick them up . . ."

Dennis Etchison

On the other side of the glass doors, Sid Caesar was even less amused by the logjam of cigarette butts on his crushed top hat. As the water rose they began to float, one disintegrating filter sloshing over the brim and catching in the knot of his limp string tie.

She forced herself to look away and crossed in front of the chairs to get to Marty, scanning the rows again. There, in the first section: an empty seat with a pair of Ray-Bans balanced on the armrest.

"Sixteen," she whispered into his ear.

"Morning, Lisa." He was about to make his introductory spiel before opening the viewing theater, while the monitors retrieved and sorted the questionnaires. "Thought you took the day off."

"Number Sixteen is missing."

He nodded at the hallway. "Check the men's room."

"I think he's outside," she said, "smoking."

"Then he's late. Send him home."

As she hurried toward the doors, the woman on the end of row four added her own questionnaire to the pile and held them out to Lisa Anne.

"Excuse me," the woman said, "but can I get a drink of water?"

Lisa Anne accepted the stack of stapled pages from her.

"If you'll wait just a moment—"

"But I have to take a pill."

"Down the hall, next to the restrooms."

"Where?"

She handed the forms to one of the other monitors.

"Angie, would you show this lady to the drinking fountain?"

Then she went on to the doors. The hinges squeaked and a stream of water poured down the glass and over the open toes of her new shoes.

Oh great, she thought.

She took the shoes off and stood under the awning while she peered through the blowing rain. The walkway along the front of the AmiDex building was empty.

"Hello?"

Bob Hope ignored her, gazing wryly across the courtyard in the direction of the adjacent apartment complex, while Dick Van Dyke and Mary Tyler Moore leaned so close to each other that their heads almost touched, about to topple off the bronze pedestals. They had not been used for ashtrays yet today, though their name-plates were etched with the faint white tracks of bird droppings. She hoped the rain would wash them clean.

"Are you out here? Mister . . . ?"

She had let Angie check them in this morning, so she did not even know Number Sixteen's name. She glanced around the courtyard, saw no movement and was about to go back inside, when she noticed someone in the parking lot.

It was a man wearing a wet trenchcoat.

So Number Sixteen had lost patience and decided to split. He did not seem to be looking for his car, however, but walked rapidly between the rows on his way to—what? The apartments beyond, apparently. Yet there was no gate in this side of the wrought-iron fence.

As she watched, another man appeared as if from nowhere. He had on a yellow raincoat and a plastic-covered hat, the kind worn by policemen or security guards. As far as she knew the parking lot was unattended. She could not imagine where had he come from, unless there was an opening in the fence, after all, and the guard had come through from the other side. He stepped out to block the way. She tried to hear what they were saying but it was impossible from this distance. There was a brief confrontation, with both men gesturing broadly, until the one in the trenchcoat gave up and walked away.

Lisa Anne shook the water out of her shoes, put them on and turned back to the glass doors.

Marty was already into his speech. She had not worked here long enough to have it memorized, but she knew he was about to mention the cash they would receive after the screening and discussion. Some of them may have been lured here by the glamor, the chance to attend a sneak preview of next season's programs, but without the promise of money there was no way to be sure anyone would show up.

The door opened a few inches and Angie stuck her head out.

"Will you get *in* here, girl?"

"Coming," said Lisa Anne.

She looked around one more time.

Now she saw a puff of smoke a few yards down, at the entrance to Public Relations.

"Is anybody there?" she called.

An eyeball showed itself at the side of the building.

Maybe this is the real Number Sixteen, she thought. Trying to get in that last nicotine fix.

"I'm sorry, but you'll have to come in now . . ."

She waited to see where his cigarette butt would fall. The statues were waiting, too. As he came toward her his hands were empty. What did he do, she wondered, eat it?

She recognized him. He had been inside, drinking coffee with the others. He was a few years older than Lisa Anne, late twenties or early thirties, good looking in a rugged, unkempt way, with his hair tied back in a ponytail and a drooping moustache, flannel shirt, tight jeans and steel-toed boots. A construction worker, she thought, a carpenter, some sort of manual labor. Why bother to test him? He probably watched football games and not much else, if he watched TV at all.

As he got closer she smelled something sweet and pungent. The unmistakable odor of marijuana lingered in his clothes. So that's what he was up to, she thought. A little attitude adjustment. I could use some of that myself right about now.

She held out her hand to invite him in from the rain, and felt her hair collapse into wet strings over her ears. She pushed it back self-consciously.

"You don't want to miss the screening," she said, forcing a smile, "do you?"

"What's it about?" he asked.

"I don't know. Honest. They don't tell me anything."

The door swung open again and Angie rolled her eyes.

"Okay, okay," said Lisa Anne.

"He can sign up for the two o'clock, if he wants."

Number Sixteen shook his head. "No way. I gotta be at work."

"It's all right, Angie."

"But he missed the audience prep . . ."

Lisa Anne looked past her. Marty was about finished. The test subjects were already shifting impatiently, bored housewives and tourists and retirees with nothing better to do, recruited from sidewalks and shopping malls and the lines in front of movie theaters, all of them here to view the pilot for a new series that would either make it to the network schedule or be sent back for retooling, based on their responses. There was a full house for this session.

Number Sixteen had not heard the instructions, so she had no choice. She was supposed to send him home.

But if the research was to mean anything, wasn't it important that every demographic be represented? The fate of the producers and writers who had labored for months or even years to get their shows this far hung in the balance, to be decided by a theoretical cross-section of the viewing public. Not everyone liked sitcoms about young urban professionals and their wacky misadventures at the office. They can't, she thought. I don't. But who ever asked me?

"Look," said Number Sixteen, "I drove a long ways to get here. You gotta at least pay me."

"He's late," said Angie. She ignored him, speaking as though he were not there. "He hasn't even filled out his questionnaire."

"Yes, he has," said Lisa Anne and ushered him inside.

The subjects were on their feet now, shuffling

into the screening room. Lisa Anne went to the check-in table.

"Did you get Number Sixteen's?" she asked.

The monitors had the forms laid out according to rows and were about to insert the piles into manila envelopes before taking them down the hall.

Marty came up behind her. "Which row, Miss Rayme?" he said officiously.

"Four, I think."

"You think?" Marty looked at the man in the plaid shirt and wrinkled his nose, as if someone in the room had just broken wind. "If his form's not here—"

"I know where it is," Lisa Anne told him and slipped behind the table.

She flipped through the pile for row four, allowing several of the questionnaires to slide onto the floor. When she knelt to pick them up, she pulled a blank one from the carton.

"Here." She stood, took a pencil and jotted *16* in the upper right-hand corner. "He forgot to put his number on it."

"We're running late, Lees . . ." Marty whispered.

She slid the forms into an envelope. "Then I'd better get these to the War Room."

On the way down the hall, she opened the envelope and withdrew the blank form, checking off random answers to the multiple-choice quiz on the first page. It was pointless, anyway, most of it a meaningless query into personal habits and lifestyle, only a smokescreen for the important questions about income and product preferences that came later. She dropped off her envelope along with the other monitors, and a humorless assistant in a short-sleeved white shirt and rimless glasses carried the envelopes from the counter to an inner room, where each form would be tallied and matched to the numbered seats in the viewing theater. On her way back, Marty intercepted her.

"Break time," he said.

"No, thanks." She drew him to one side, next to the drinking fountain. "I got one for you. *S.H.A.M.*"

"*M.A.S.H.*," he said immediately.

"Okay, try this. *Finders*."

He pondered for a second. "*Friends?*"

"You're good," she said.

"No, I'm not. You're easy. Well, time to do my thing."

At the other end of the hall, the reception room was empty and the doors to the viewing theater were already closed.

"Which thing is that?" she said playfully.

"That thing I do, before they fall asleep."

"Ooh, can I watch?"

She propped her back against the wall and waited for him to move in, to pin her there until she could not get away unless she dropped to her knees and crawled between his legs.

"Not today, Lisa."

"How come?"

"This one sucks. Big time."

"What's the title?"

"I don't know."

"Then how do you know it sucks?"

"Hey, it's not my fault, okay?"

For some reason he had become evasive, defensive. His face was now a smooth mask, the skin pulled back tautly, the only prominent features his teeth and nervous, shining eyes. Like a shark's face, she thought. A residue of deodorant soap rose to the surface of his skin and vaporized, expanding outward on waves of body heat. She drew a breath and knew that she needed to be somewhere else, away from him.

"Sorry," she said.

He avoided her eyes and ducked into the men's room.

What did I say? she wondered, and went on to the reception area.

A list of subjects for the next session was already laid out on the table, ninety minutes early. The other monitors were killing time in the chairs, chatting over coffee and snacks from the machines.

Lisa Anne barely knew them. This was only her second week and she was not yet a part of their circle. One had been an editorial assistant at the *L.A. Weekly*, two were junior college students, and the others had answered the same classified ad she had seen in the trades. She considered crashing the conversation. It would be a chance to rest her feet and dry out. The soggy new shoes still pinched her toes and the suit she'd had to buy for the job was damp and steamy and scratched her skin like a hair shirt. She felt ridiculous in this uniform, but it was necessary to show people like Marty that she could play by their rules, at least until she got what she needed. At home she would probably be working on yet another sculpture this morning, trying to get the face right, with a gob of clay in one hand and a joint in the other and the stereo cranked up to the max. But living that way hadn't gotten her any closer to the truth. She couldn't put it off any longer. There were some things she had to find out or she would go mad.

She smiled at the monitors.

Except for Angie they barely acknowledged her, continuing their conversation as though she were not there.

They know, she thought. They must.

How much longer till Marty saw through her game? She had him on her side, but the tease would play out soon enough unless she let it go further, and she couldn't bear the thought of that. She only needed him long enough to find the answer, and then she would walk away.

She went to the glass doors.

The rain had stopped and soon the next group would begin gathering outside. The busts of the television stars in the courtyard were ready, Red Buttons and George Gobel and Steve Allen and Lucille Ball with her eyebrows arched in perpetual wonderment, waiting to meet their fans. It was all that was left for them now.

Angie came up next to her.

"Hey, girl."

"Hey yourself."

"The lumberjack. He a friend of yours?"

"Number Sixteen?"

"The one with the buns."

"I never saw him before."

"Oh." Angie took a bite of an oatmeal cookie and brushed the crumbs daintily from her mouth. "Nice."

"I suppose. If you like that sort of thing."

"Here." She offered Lisa Anne the napkin. "You look like you're melting."

She took it and wiped the back of her neck, then squeezed out the ends of her hair, as a burst of laughter came from the theater. That meant Marty had already gone in through the side entrance to warm them up.

"Excuse me," she said. "It's showtime."

Angie followed her to the hall. "You never miss one, do you?"

"Not yet."

"Aren't they boring? I mean, it's not like they're hits or anything."

"Most of them are pretty lame," Lisa Anne admitted.

"So why watch?"

"I have to find out."

"Don't tell me. What Marty's really like?"

"Please."

"Then why?"

"I've got to know why some shows make it," she said, "and some don't."

"Oh, you want to get into the biz?"

"No. But I used to know someone who was. See you."

I shouldn't have said that, she thought as she opened the unmarked door in the hall.

The observation booth was dark and narrow with a half-dozen padded chairs facing a two-way mirror. On the other side of the mirror, the test subjects sat in rows of theater seats under several 36-inch television sets suspended from the ceiling.

She took the second chair from the end.

In the viewing theater, Marty was explaining how to use the dials wired into the armrests. They were calibrated from zero to ten with a plastic knob in the center. During the screening the subjects were to rotate the knobs, indicating how much they liked what they saw. Their responses would be recorded and the results then analyzed to help the networks decide whether the show was ready for broadcast.

Lisa Anne watched Marty as he paced, doing his schtick. He had told her that he once worked at a comedy traffic school, and she could see why. He had them in the palm of his hand. Their eyes followed his every move, like hypnotized chickens waiting to be fed. His routine was corny but with just the right touch of hipness to make them feel like insiders. He concluded by reminding them of the fifty dollars cash they would receive after the screening and the discussion. Then, when the lights went down and the tape began to roll, Marty stepped to the back and slipped into the hall. As he entered the observation booth, the audience was applauding.

"Good group this time," he said, dropping into the chair next to hers.

"You always know just what to say."

"I do, don't I?" he said, leaning forward to turn on a tiny 12-inch set below the mirror.

She saw their faces flicker in the blue glow of the cathode ray tubes while the opening titles came up.

The show was something called *Dario, You So Crazy!* She sighed and sat back, studying their expressions while keeping one eye on the TV screen. It wouldn't be long before she felt his hand on her forearm as he moved in, telling her what he really thought of the audience, how stupid they were, every last one, down to the little old ladies and the kindly grandfathers and the working men and women who were no more or less ordinary than he was under his Perry Ellis suit and silk tie. Then his breath in her hair and his fingers scraping her pantyhose as if tapping out a message on her knee and perhaps today, this time, he would attempt to deliver that message, while she offered breathless quips to let him know how clever he was and how lucky she felt to be here. She shuddered and turned her cheek to him in the dark.

"Who's that actor?" she said.

"Some Italian guy. I saw him in a movie. He's not so bad, if he could learn to talk English."

She recognized the co-star. It was Rowan Atkinson, the slight, bumbling everyman from that British TV series on PBS.

"Mr. Bean!" she said.

"Roberto Begnino," Marty corrected, reading from the credits.

"I mean the other one. This is going to be good . . ."

"I thought you were on your break," said Marty.

"This is more important."

He stared at her transparent reflection in the two-way mirror.

"You were going to take the day off."

"No, I wasn't."

The pilot was a comedy about an eccentric Italian film director who had come to America in search of fame and fortune. Mr. Bean played his shy, inept manager. They shared an expensive rented villa in the Hollywood Hills. Just now they were desperate to locate an actress to pose as Dario's wife, so that he could obtain a green card and find work before they both ran out of money.

She immediately grasped the premise and its potential.

It was inspired. Benigno's abuse of the language would generate countless hilarious misunderstandings; coupled with his manager's charming incompetence, the result might be a television classic, thanks in no small measure to the brilliant casting. How could it miss? All they needed was a good script. She realized that her mind had drifted long enough to miss the screenwriter's name. The only credit left was the show's creator/producer, one Barry E. Tormé. Probably the son of that old singer, she thought. What was his name? Mel. Apparently he had fathered a show-business dynasty. The other son, Tracy, was a successful TV writer; he had even created a science-fiction series at Fox that lasted for a couple of seasons. Why had she never heard of brother Barry? He was obviously a pro.

She sat forward, fascinated to see the first episode.

"*Me, Dario!*" Benigno crowed into a gold-trimmed telephone, the third time it had rung in less than a minute. It was going to be his signature bit.

"*O, I Dream!*" she said.

"Huh?"

"The line, Marty. Got you."

The letters rearranged themselves automatically in her mind. It was child's play. She had almost expected him to come up with it first. They had kept the game going since her first day at AmiDex, when she pointed out that his full name was an anagram for *Marty licks on me*. It got his attention.

"You can stop with the word shit," he said.

He sounded irritated, which surprised her. "I thought you liked it."

"What's up with that, anyway?"

"It's a reflex," she said. "I can't help it. My father taught me when I was little."

"Well, it's getting old."

She turned to his profile in the semidarkness, his pale, clean-shaven face and short, neat hair as two-dimensional as a cartoon cutout from the back of a cereal box.

Dennis Etchison

"You know, Marty, I was thinking. Could you show me the War Room sometime?" She moved her leg closer to his. "Just you and me, when everybody's gone. So I could see how it works."

"How what works?"

She let her hand brush his knee. "Everything. The really big secrets."

"Such as?"

"I don't know." Had she said too much? "But if I'm going to work here, I should know more about the company. What makes a hit, for example. Maybe you could tell me. You explain things so well."

"Why *did* you come here?"

The question caught her offguard. "I needed a job."

"Plenty of jobs out there," he snapped. "What is it, you got a script to sell?"

The room was cold and her feet were numb. Now she wanted to be out of here. The other chairs were dim, bulky shapes, like half-reclining corpses, as if she and Marty were not alone in the room.

"Sorry," she said.

"I told you to stay home today."

No, he hadn't. "You *want* me to take the day off?"

He did not answer.

"Do you think I need it? Or is there something special about today?"

The door in the back of the room opened. It connected to the hall that led to the other sections of the building and the War Room itself, where even now the audience response was being recorded and analyzed by a team of market researchers. A hulking figure stood there in silhouette. She could not see his features. He hesitated for a moment, then came all the way in, plunging the room into darkness again, and then there were only the test subjects and their flickering faces opposite her through the smoked glass. The man took a seat at the other end of the row.

"That you, Mickleson?"

At the sound of his voice Marty sat up straight.

"Yes, sir."

"I thought so. Who's she?"

"One of the girls—Annalise. She was just leaving."

Then Marty leaned close to her and whispered:

"Will you get out?"

She was not supposed to be here. The shape at the end of the row must have been the big boss. Marty had known he was coming; that was why he wanted her gone. This was the first time anyone had joined them in the booth. It meant the show was important. The executives listened up when a hit came along.

"Excuse me," she said, and left the observation booth.

She wanted very much to see the rest of the show. Now she would have to wait till it hit the airwaves. Was there a way for her to eavesdrop on the discussion later, after the screening?

In the hall, she listened for the audience reaction. Just now there must have been a lull in the action, with blank tape inserted to represent a commercial break, because there was dead silence from the theater.

She was all the way to the reception area before she realized what he had called her.

Annalise.

It was an anagram for Lisa Anne, the name she had put on her application—and, incredibly, it was the right one. Somehow he had hit it. Had he done so naturally, without thinking, as in their word games? Or did he know?

Busted, she thought.

She crossed to the glass doors, ready to make her break.

Then she thought, So he knows my first name. So what? It's not like it would mean anything to him, even if he were to figure out the rest of it.

She decided that she had been paranoid to use a pseudonym in the first place. If she had told the truth, would anybody care? Technically AmiDex could disqualify her, but the family connection was so many years ago that the name had probably been forgotten by now. In fact she was sure it had. That was the point. That was why she was here.

Outside, the rain had let up. A few of the next hour's subjects were already wandering this way across the courtyard. Only one, a woman with a shopping bag and a multi-colored scarf over her hair, bothered to raise her head to look at the statues.

It was disturbing to see the greats treated with such disrespect.

All day long volunteers gathered outside at the appointed hour, smoking and drinking sodas and eating food they had brought with them, and when they went in they left the remains scattered among the statues, as if the history of the medium and its stars meant nothing to them. Dinah Shore and Carol Burnett and Red Skelton with his clown nose, all nothing more than a part of the landscape now, like the lampposts, like the trash cans that no one used. The sun fell on them, and the winds and the rains and the grafitti and the discarded wads of chewing gum and the pissing of dogs on the place where their feet should have been, and there was nothing for any of them to do but suffer these things with quiet dignity, like the fallen dead in a veterans' cemetery. One day the burdens of their immortality, the birdshit and

Dennis Etchison

the cigarette butts and the MacDonald's wrappers, might become too much for them to bear and the ground would shake as giants walked the earth again, but for now they could only wait, because that day was not yet here.

"How was it?" said Angie.

"The show? Oh, it was great. Really."

"Then why aren't you in there?"

"It's too cold." She hugged her sides. "When does the grounds crew get here?"

"Uh, you lost me."

"Maintenance. The gardeners. How often do they come?"

"You're putting me on, right?"

She felt her face flush. "Then I'll do it."

"Do—?"

"Clean up. It's a disgrace. Don't you think so?"

"Sure, Lisa. Anything you say . . ."

She started outside, and got only a few paces when the sirens began. She counted four squad cars with the name of a private security company stenciled on the doors. They screeched to a halt in the parking lot and several officers jumped out. Did one of them really have his gun drawn?

"Oh, God," said Angie.

"What's going on?"

"It's the complex. They don't like people taking pictures."

Now she saw that the man in the dark trenchcoat had returned. This time he had brought a van with a remote broadcasting dish on top. The guards held him against the side, under the call letters for a local TV station and the words *EYEBALL NEWS*.

When a cameraman climbed down from the back to object they handcuffed him.

"Who doesn't like it?"

"AmiDex," Angie said solemnly. "They own it all." She waved her hand to include the building, the courtyard, the parking lot and the fenced-in apartments. "Somebody from *Hard Copy* tried to shoot here last month. They confiscated the film. It's off-limits."

"But why?"

"All I know is, there must be some very important people in those condos."

"In *this* neighborhood?"

She couldn't imagine why any VIP's would want to live here. The complex was a lower-middle-class housing development, walled in and protected from the deteriorating streets nearby. It had probably been on this corner since the fifties. She could understand AmiDex buying real estate in the San Fernando Valley instead of the overpriced Westside, but why the aging apartments? The only reason might be so that they could expand their testing facility one day. Meanwhile, why not tear them down? With its spiked iron fences the complex looked like a fortress sealed off against the outside world. There was even barbed wire on top of the walls.

Before she could ask any more questions, the doors to the theater opened. She glanced back and saw Marty leading the audience down the hall for the post-screening discussion.

She followed, eager to hear the verdict.

The boys in the white shirts were no longer at the counter. They were in the War Room, marking up long rolls of paper like doctors charting the vital signs in an intensive care ward. Lights blinked across a bank of electronic equipment, as many rack-mounted modules as there were seats in the theater, with dials and connecting cables that fed into the central computer. She heard circuits humming and the ratcheting whir of a wide-mouthed machine as it disgorged graphs that resembled polygraph tests printed in blood-red ink.

She came to the next section of the hall, as the last head vanished through a doorway around the first turn.

The discussion room was small and bright with rows of desks and acoustic tiles in the ceiling. It reminded her of the classrooms at UCLA, where she had taken a course in Media Studies, before discovering that they didn't have any answers, either. She merged with the group and slumped down in the back row, behind the tallest person she could find.

Marty remained on his feet, pacing.

"Now," he said, "it's your turn. Hollywood is listening! How many of you would rate—" He consulted his clipboard. "—*Dario, You So Crazy!* as one of the best programs you've ever seen?"

She waited for the hands to go up. She could not see any from here. The tall man blocked her view and if she moved her head Marty might spot her.

"Okay. How many would say 'very good'?"

There must not have been many because he went right on to the next question.

" 'Fair'?"

She closed her eyes and listened to the rustle of coat sleeves and wondered if she had heard the question correctly.

"And how many 'poor'?"

That had to be everyone else. Even the tall man in front of her raised his arm. She recognized his plaid shirt. It was Number Sixteen.

Marty made a notation.

"Okay, great. What was your favorite scene?"

The silence was deafening.

"You won't be graded on this! There's no right or wrong answer. I remember once, when my junior-high English teacher . . ."

He launched into a story to loosen them up. It was about a divorced woman, an escaped sex maniac and a telephone call to the police. She

Dennis Etchison

recognized it as a very old dirty joke. Astonishingly he left off the punchline. The audience responded anyway. He had his timing down pat. Or was it that they laughed *because* they knew what was coming? Did that make it even funnier?

The less original the material, she thought, the more they like it. It makes them feel comfortable.

And if that's true, so is the reverse.

She noticed that there was a two-way mirror in this room, too, along the far wall. Was anyone following the discussion from the other side? If so, there wasn't much to hear. Nobody except Marty had anything to say. They were bored stiff, waiting for their money. It would take something more than the show they had just seen to hold them, maybe *Wrestling's Biggest Bleeps, Bloopers and Bodyslams* or *America's Zaniest Surveillance Tapes*. Now she heard a door slam in the hall. The executives had probably given up and left the observation room.

"What is the matter with you people?"

The woman with the multi-colored scarf hunched around to look at her, as Marty tried to see who had spoken.

"In the back row. Number . . ."

"You're right," she said too loudly. "It's not poor, or fair, or excellent. It's a *great* show! Better than anything I've seen in years. Since—"

"Yes?" Marty changed his position, zeroing in on her voice. "Would you mind speaking up? This is your chance to be heard . . ."

"Since *The Fuzzy Family*. Or *The Funnyboner*." She couldn't help mentioning the titles. Her mouth was open now and the truth was coming out and there was no way to stop it.

Marty said, "What network were they on?"

"CBS. They were canceled in the first season."

"But you remember them?"

"They were brilliant."

"Can you tell us why?"

"Because of my father. He created them both."

Marty came to the end of the aisle and finally saw her. His face fell. In the silence she heard other voices, arguing in the hall. She hoped it was not the people who had made *Dario, You So Crazy!* If so, they had to be hurting right now. She felt for them, bitterness and despair and rage welling up in her own throat.

"May I see you outside?" he said.

"No, you may not."

The hell with Marty, AmiDex and her job here. There was no secret as to why some shows made it and other, better ones did not. Darwin was wrong. He hadn't figured on the networks. They had continued to lower their sights until the audience devolved right along with them, so that any ray of hope was snuffed out, over-shadowed by the crap around it. And market research and the ratings system held onto their positions by telling them what they wanted to hear, that the low-rent talent they had under contract was good enough, by testing the wrong people for the wrong reasons, people who were too numb to care about a pearl among the pebbles. It was a perfect, closed loop.

"*Now*, Miss Rayme."

"That isn't my name." Didn't he get it yet? "My father was Robert Mayer. The man who wrote and produced *Wagons, Ho!*"

It was TV's first western comedy and it made television history. After that he struggled to come up with another hit, but every new show was either canceled or rejected outright. His name meant nothing to the bean-counters. All they could see was the bottom line. As far as they were concerned he owed them a fortune for the failures they had bankrolled. If he had been an entertainer who ran up a debt in Vegas, he would have had to stay there, working it off at the rate of two shows a night, forever. The only thing that gave her satisfaction was the knowledge that they would never collect. One day when she was ten he had a massive heart attack on the set and was whisked away in a blue ambulance and he never came home again.

"Folks, thanks for your time," Marty said. "If you'll return to the lobby . . ."

She had studied his notes and scripts, trying to understand why he failed. She loved them all. They were genuinely funny, the very essence of her father, with his quirky sense of humor and extravagant sight gags—as original and inventive as *Dario, You So Crazy!* Which was a failure, too. Of course. She lowered her head onto the desktop and began to weep.

"Hold up," said Number Sixteen.

"Your pay's ready. Fifty dollars cash." Marty held the door wide. "There's another group coming in . . ."

The lumberjack refused to stand. "Let her talk. I remember *Wagons, Ho!* It was all right."

He turned around in his seat and gave her a wink as she raised her head.

"Thank you," she said softly. "It doesn't matter, now."

She got to her feet with the others and pushed her way out. Farther down the hall, another door clicked shut. It was marked Green Room. She guessed that the executives from the other side of the mirror had decided to finish their argument in private.

Marty grabbed her elbow.

"I told you to stay home."

"You're hurting me," she said.

"But you just wouldn't take the hint, would you?"

"About what?"

"You can pick up your check in Payroll."

"Get your hands off me."

Number Sixteen came up next to her. "You got a problem here?"

"Not anymore," she said.

"Your pay's up front, cowboy," Marty told him.

"You sure you're okay?" asked Number Sixteen.

"I am now."

Marty shook his head sadly.

"I'll tell them to make it for the full two weeks. I liked you, you know? I really did."

Then he turned and walked the audience back to the lobby.

Farther down the hall, she saw Human Resources, where she had gone the first day for her interview, and beyond that Public Relations and Payroll. She didn't care about her check but there was a security door at the end. It would let her out directly into the courtyard.

Number Sixteen followed her.

"I was thinking. If you want some lunch, I've got my car."

"So do I," she said, walking faster.

Then she thought, Why not? Me, with a lumberjack. I'll be watching Martha Stewart while

he hammers his wood and lays his pipe or whatever he does all day, and he'll come home and
watch hockey games and I'll stay loaded and sit
up every night to see *Wagons, Ho!* on the Nos-
talgia Channel and we'll go on that way, like a
sitcom. He'll take care of me. And in time I'll
forget everything. All I have to do is say yes.

He was about to turn back.

"Okay," she said.

"What?"

"This way. There's an exit to the parking lot,
down here."

Before they could get to it the steel door at
the end swung open.

The rain had stopped and a burst of clear
light from outside reflected off the polished
floor, distorting the silhouette of the figure
standing there. A tall woman in a designer suit
entered from the grounds. Behind her, the last
of the private security cars drove off. The Eyeball News truck was gone.

"All set," the woman said into a flip-phone,
and went briskly to the door marked Green
Room.

Voices came from within, rising to an emo-
tional pitch. Then the voices receded as the
door clicked shut.

There was something in the tone of the argument that got to her. She couldn't make out
the words but one of the voices was close to

279

pleading. It was painful to hear. She thought of her father and the desperate meetings he must have had, years ago. When the door whispered open again, two men in gray suits stepped out into the hall, holding a third man between them.

It had to be the producer of the pilot.

She wanted to go to him and take his hands and look into his eyes and tell him that they were wrong. He was too talented to listen to them. What did they know? There were other networks, cable, foreign markets, features, if only he could break free of them and move on. He had to. She would be waiting and so would millions of others, an invisible audience whose opinions were never counted, as if they did not exist, but who were out there, she was sure. The ones who remembered *Wagons, Ho!* and *The Funnyboner* and *The Fuzzy Family* and would faithfully tune in other programs with the same quirky sensibility, if they had the choice.

He looked exhausted. The suits had him in their grip, supporting his weight between them, as if carrying a drunk to a waiting cab. What was his name? Terry Something. Or Barry. That was it. She saw him go limp. He had the body of a middle-aged man.

"Please," he said in a cracking voice, "this is the one, you'll see. *Please* . . ."

"Mr. Tormé?" she called out, remembering

his name. The letters shuffled like a deck of cards in her mind and settled into a new pattern. It was a reflex she could not control, ever since she had learned the game from her father so many years ago, before the day they took him away and told his family that he was dead.

Barry E. Tormé, she thought.

You could spell a lot of words with those letters.

Even . . .

Robert Mayer.

He turned slightly, and she saw the familiar nose and chin she had tried so many times to reproduce, working from fading photographs and the shadow pictures in her mind. The two men continued to drag him forward. His shoes left long black skidmarks on the polished floor. Then they lifted him off his feet and he was lost in the light.

Outside the door, a blue van was waiting.

They dumped him in and locked the tailgate. Beyond the parking lot lay the walled compound, where the razor wire gleamed like hungry teeth atop the barricades and forgotten people lived out lives as bleak as unsold pilots and there was no way out for any of them until the cameras rolled again on another hit.

Milton Berle and Johnny Carson and Jackie Gleason watched mutely, stars who had become famous by speaking the words put into their mouths by others, by men who had no monuments to honor them, not here or anywhere else.

Now she knew the real reason she had come to this place. There was something missing. When she finished her sculpture there would be a new face for the courtyard, one who deserved a statue of his own. And this time she would get it right.

The steel door began to close.

Sorry, Daddy! she thought as the rain started again outside. I'm sorry, sorry. . . .

"Wait." Number Sixteen put on his Ray-Bans. "I gotta get my pay first. You want to come with me?"

Yes, we could do that. Simple. All we do is turn and run the other way, like Lucy and Desi, like Dario and Mr. Bean, bumbling along to a private hell of our own. What's the difference?

"No," she said.

"I thought—"

"I'm sorry. I can't."

"Why not?"

"I just . . . can't."

She ran instead toward the light at the end, hoping to see the face in the van clearly one last time as it drove away, before the men in the suits could stop her.

The Horror Writers Association presents:
THE MUSEUM OF HORRORS
edited by Dennis Etchison

A special hardcover edition featuring all new stories by:

PETER STRAUB
JOYCE CAROL OATES
RICHARD LAYMON
BENTLEY LITTLE
RAMSEY CAMPBELL

*And: Peter Atkins, Melanie Tem, Tom Piccirilli,
Darren O. Godfrey, Joel Lane, Gordon Linzer, Conrad Williams,
Th. Metzger, Susan Fry, Charles L. Grant, Lisa Morton,
William F. Nolan, Robert Devereaux, and S. P. Somtow.*

"The connoisseur of the macabre will find a feast on this table."
—Tapestry Magazine

Dorchester Publishing Co., Inc.
P.O. Box 6640
Wayne, PA 19087-8640

0-8439-4928-7
$24.00 US/ $34.95 CAN

Please add $4.00 for shipping and handling NY residents, please add appropriate sales tax. No cash, stamps, or C.O.D.s. All orders take 7-10 days to be fulfilled after they are received by our order department. Canadian orders require $5.00 for shipping and must be paid in U.S. dollars. Prices and availability subject to change. Payment must accompany all orders.

Name _____

Address _____

City _____ State_____ Zip _____

E-mail _____

I have enclosed $ _____ in payment for the checked book(s). **Payment must accompany all orders.**

__Check here for a FREE catalog

Check out our website at www.dorchesterpub.com
for even more information on your favorite books and authors.

Elizabeth Massie
Wire Mesh Mothers

It all starts with the best of intentions. Kate McDolen, an elementary school teacher, knows she has to protect little eight-year-old Mistie from parents who are making her life a living hell. So Kate packs her bags, quietly picks up Mistie after school one day and sets off with her toward what she thinks will be a new life. How can she know she is driving headlong into a nightmare?

The nightmare begins when Tony jumps into the passenger seat of Kate's car, waving a gun. Tony is a dangerous girl, more dangerous than anyone could dream. She doesn't admire anything except violence and cruelty, and she has very different plans in mind for Kate and little Mistie. The cross-country trip that follows will turn into a one-way journey to fear, desperation . . . and madness.

___4869-8 $5.99 US/$6.99 CAN

Dorchester Publishing Co., Inc.
P.O. Box 6640
Wayne, PA 19087-8640

Please add $1.75 for shipping and handling for the first book and $.50 for each book thereafter. NY, NYC, and PA residents, please add appropriate sales tax. No cash, stamps, or C.O.D.s. All orders shipped within 6 weeks via postal service book rate. Canadian orders require $2.00 extra postage and must be paid in U.S. dollars through a U.S. banking facility.

Name_____
Address_____
City_____ State_____ Zip_____
I have enclosed $ _____ in payment for the checked book(s).
Payment <u>must</u> accompany all orders. ❑ Please send a free catalog.
       CHECK OUT OUR WEBSITE! www.dorchesterpub.com

T. M. WRIGHT
Sleepeasy

Harry Briggs led a fairly normal life. He had a good job, a nice house, and a beautiful wife named Barbara, with whom he was very much in love. Then he died. That's when Harry's story really begins. That's when he finds himself in a strange little town called Silver Lake. In Silver Lake nothing is normal. In Silver Lake Harry has become a detective, tough and silent, hot on the trail of a missing woman and a violent madman. But the town itself is an enigma. It's a shadowy twilight town, filled with ghostly figures that seem to be playing according to someone else's rules. Harry has unwittingly brought other things with him to this eerie realm. Things like uncertainty, fear . . . and death.

___4864-7 $5.99 US/$6.99 CAN

SIMON CLARK

Darkness Demands

Life looks good for John Newton. He lives in the quiet village of Skelbrooke with his family. He has a new home and a successful career writing true crime books. He never gives a thought to the vast nearby cemetery known as the Necropolis. He never wonders what might lurk there.

Then the letters begin to arrive in the dead of night demanding trivial offerings—chocolate, beer, toys. At first John dismisses the notes as a prank. But he soon learns the hard way that they're not. For there is an ancient entity that resides beneath the Necropolis that has the power to demand things. And the power to punish those foolish enough to refuse.

___4898-1 $5.99 US/$6.99 CAN

Dorchester Publishing Co., Inc.
P.O. Box 6640
Wayne, PA 19087-8640

Please add $1.75 for shipping and handling for the first book and $.50 for each book thereafter. NY, NYC, and PA residents, please add appropriate sales tax. No cash, stamps, or C.O.D.s. All orders shipped within 6 weeks via postal service book rate. Canadian orders require $2.00 extra postage and must be paid in U.S. dollars through a U.S. banking facility.

Name_____
Address_____
City_____ State_____ Zip_____
I have enclosed $ _____ in payment for the checked book(s).
Payment must accompany all orders. ❑ Please send a free catalog.
CHECK OUT OUR WEBSITE! *www.dorchesterpub.com*

SIMON CLARK

Blood Crazy

Saturday is a normal day. People go shopping. To the movies. Everything is just as it should be. But not for long. By Sunday, civilization is in ruins. Adults have become murderously insane. One by one they become infected with a crazed, uncontrollable urge to slaughter the young—even their own children. Especially their own children.

Will this be the way the world ends, in waves of madness and carnage? What will be left of our world as we know it? And who, if anyone, will survive? Terror follows terror in this apocalyptic nightmare vision by one of the most powerful talents in modern horror fiction. Prepare yourself for mankind's final days of fear.

__4825-6 $5.99 US/$6.99 CAN

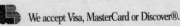